A Dream of John Ball

AND

A King's Lesson

A Dream of John Ball

AND

A King's Lesson

WILLIAM MORRIS

ÆGYPAN PRESS

Text from the 1903 Longmans, Green, and Co. edition.

A Dream of John Ball
and
A King's Lesson
A publication of
ÆGYPAN PRESS

www.aegypan.com

Chapter I

THE MEN OF KENT

Sometimes I am rewarded for fretting myself so much about present matters by a quite unasked-for pleasant dream. I mean when I am asleep. This dream is as it were a present of an architectural peep-show. I see some beautiful and noble building new made, as it were for the occasion, as clearly as if I were awake; not vaguely or absurdly, as often happens in dreams, but with all the detail clear and reasonable. Some Elizabethan house with its scrap of earlier fourteenth-century building, and its later degradations of Queen Anne and Silly Billy and Victoria, marring but not destroying it, in an old village once a clearing amid the sandy woodlands of Sussex. Or an old and unusually curious church, much churchwardened, and beside it a fragment of fifteenth-century domestic architecture amongst the not unpicturesque lath and plaster of an Essex farm, and looking natural enough among the sleepy elms and the meditative hens scratching about in the litter of the farmyard, whose trodden yellow straw comes up to the very jambs of the richly carved Norman doorway of the church. Or sometimes 'tis a splendid collegiate church, untouched by restoring parson and architect, standing amid an island of shapely trees and flower-beset cottages of thatched grey stone and cob, amidst the narrow stretch of bright green water-meadows that wind between the sweeping Wiltshire downs, so well beloved of William Cobbett. Or some new-seen and yet familiar cluster of houses in a grey village of the upper Thames over topped by the delicate tracery of a fourteenth-century church; or even sometimes the very buildings of the past untouched by the degradation of the sordid utilitarianism that cares not and knows not of beauty and history: as once, when I was journeying (in a dream of the night) down the well-remembered reaches of the Thames betwixt Streatley and Walling-ford, where the foothills of the White Horse fall back from the broad stream, I came upon a clear-seen mediæval town standing up with roof and tower and spire within its walls, grey and ancient, but untouched from the days of its builders of old. All this I have seen in the dreams of the night clearer than I can force myself to see them in dreams of the day. So that it would have been nothing new to me the other night to fall into an architectural dream if that were all, and yet I have to tell of things strange and new that befell me after I had fallen asleep. I had begun my sojourn in the Land of Nod by a very confused attempt to conclude that it was all right for me to have an engage-ment to lecture at Manchester and Mitcham Fair Green at half-past eleven at night on one and the same Sun-day, and that I could manage pretty well. And then I had gone on to try to make the best of addressing a large open-air audience in the costume I was really then wearing — to wit, my night-shirt, reinforced for the dream occasion by a pair of braceless trousers. The consciousness of this fact so bothered me, that the earnest faces of my audience — who would *not* notice it, but were clearly preparing terrible anti-Socialist posers for me — began to fade away and my dream grew thin, and I awoke (as I thought) to find myself lying on a strip of wayside waste by an oak copse just outside a country village.

I got up and rubbed my eyes and looked about me, and the landscape seemed unfamiliar to me, though it was, as to the lie of the land, an ordinary English low-country, swelling into rising ground here and there. The road was narrow, and I was convinced that it was a piece of Roman road from its straightness. Copses were scattered over the country, and there were signs of two or three villages and hamlets in sight besides the one near me, between which and me there was some orchard-land, where the early apples were beginning to redden on the trees. Also, just on the other side of the road and the ditch which ran along it, was a small close of about a quarter of an acre, neatly hedged with quick, which was nearly full of white poppies, and, as far as I could see for the hedge, had also a good few rose-bushes of the bright-red nearly single kind, which I had heard are the ones from which rose-water used to be distilled. Otherwise the land was quite unhedged, but all under tillage of various kinds, mostly in small strips. From the other side of a copse not far off rose a tall spire white and brand-new, but at once bold in outline and unaffectedly graceful and also distinctly English in character. This, together with the unhedged tillage and a certain unwonted trimness and handiness about the enclosures of the garden and orchards, puzzled me for a minute or two, as I did not understand, new as the spire was, how it could have been designed by a modern architect; and I was of course used to the hedged tillage and tumbledown

bankrupt-looking surroundings of our modern agri-
culture. So that the gardenlike neatness and trimness
of everything surprised me. But after a minute or two
that surprise left me entirely; and if what I saw and
heard afterwards seems strange to you, remember that
it did not seem strange to me at the time, except where
now and again I shall tell you of it. Also, once for all,
if I were to give you the very words of those who spoke
to me you would scarcely understand them, although
their language was English too, and at the time I could
understand them at once.

Well, as I stretched myself and turned my face toward
the village, I heard horse-hoofs on the road, and presently a man and horse showed on the other end of the
stretch of road and drew near at a swinging trot with
plenty of clash of metal. The man soon came up to
me, but paid me no more heed than throwing me a
nod. He was clad in armor of mingled steel and leather,
a sword girt to his side, and over his shoulder a long-
handled billhook. His armor was fantastic in form and
well wrought; but by this time I was quite used to the
strangeness of him, and merely muttered to myself,
"He is coming to summon the squire to the leet;" so I
turned toward the village in good earnest. Nor, again,
was I surprised at my own garments, although I might
well have been from their unwontedness. I was dressed
in a black cloth gown reaching to my ankles, neatly
embroidered about the collar and cuffs, with wide
sleeves gathered in at the wrists; a hood with a sort of
bag hanging down from it was on my head, a broad
red leather girdle round my waist, on one side of which
hung a pouch embroidered very prettily and a case
made of hard leather chased with a hunting scene,
which I knew to be a pen and ink case; on the other
side a small sheath-knife, only an arm in case of dire
necessity.

Well, I came into the village, where I did not see (nor by this time expected to see) a single modern building, although many of them were nearly new, notably the church, which was large, and quite ravished my heart with its extreme beauty, elegance, and fitness. The chancel of this was so new that the dust of the stone still lay white on the midsummer grass beneath the carvings of the windows. The houses were almost all built of oak frame-work filled with cob or plaster well whitewashed; though some had their lower stories of rubble-stone, with their windows and doors of well-molded freestone. There was much curious and inventive carving about most of them; and though some were old and much worn, there was the same look of deftness and trimness, and even beauty, about every detail in them which I noticed before in the field-work. They were all roofed with oak shingles, mostly grown as grey as stone; but one was so newly built that its roof was yet pale and yellow. This was a corner house, and the corner post of it had a carved niche wherein stood a gaily painted figure holding an anchor — St. Clement to wit, as the dweller in the house was a blacksmith. Half a stone's throw from the east end of the church-yard wall was a tall cross of stone, new like the church, the head beautifully carved with a crucifix amidst leafage. It stood on a set of wide stone steps, octagonal in shape, where three roads from other villages met and formed a wide open space on which a thousand people or more could stand together with no great crowding.

All this I saw, and also that there was a goodish many people about, women and children, and a few old men at the doors, many of them somewhat gaily clad, and that men were coming into the village street by the other end to that by which I had entered, by twos and threes, most of them carrying what I could see were bows in cases of linen yellow with wax or oil; they had quivers at their backs, and most of them a short sword by their left side, and a pouch and knife on the right; they were mostly dressed in red or brightish green or blue cloth jerkins, with a hood on the head generally of another color. As they came nearer I saw that the cloth of their garments was somewhat coarse, but stout and serviceable. I knew, somehow, that they had been shooting at the butts, and, indeed, I could still hear a noise of men thereabout, and even now and again when the wind set from that quarter the twang of the bowstring and the plump of the shaft in the target.

I leaned against the churchyard wall and watched these men, some of whom went straight into their houses and some loitered about still; they were rough-looking fellows, tall and stout, very black some of them, and some red-haired, but most had hair burned by the sun into the color of tow; and, indeed, they were all burned and tanned and freckled variously. Their arms and buckles and belts and the finishings and hems of their garments were all what we should now call beautiful, rough as the men were; nor in their speech was any of that drawling snarl or thick vulgarity which one is used to hear from laborers in civilization; not that they talked like gentlemen either, but full and round and bold, and they were merry and good-tempered enough; I could see that, though I felt shy and timid amongst them.

Once of them strode up to me across the road, a man some six feet high, with a short black beard and black eyes and berry-brown skin, with a huge bow in his hand bare of the case, a knife, a pouch, and a short hatchet, all clattering together at his girdle.

"Well, friend," said he, "thou lookest partly mazed; what tongue hast thou in thine head?"

"A tongue that can tell rhymes," said I.

"So I thought," said he. "Thirstest thou any?"

"Yea, and hunger," said I.

And therewith my hand went into my purse, and came out again with but a few small and thin silver coins with a cross stamped on each, and three pellets in each corner of the cross. The man grinned.

"Aha!" said he, "is it so? Never heed it, mate. It shall be a song for a supper this fair Sunday evening. But first, whose man art thou?"

"No one's man," said I, reddening angrily; "I am my own master."

He grinned again.

"Nay, that's not the custom of England, as one time belike it will be. Methinks thou comest from heaven down, and hast had a high place there too."

He seemed to hesitate a moment, and then leant forward and whispered in my ear: *"John the Miller, that ground small, small, small,"* and stopped and winked at me, and from between my lips without my mind forming any meaning came the words, *"The king's son of heaven shall pay for all."*

He let his bow fall on to his shoulder, caught my right hand in his and gave it a great grip, while his left hand fell among the gear at his belt, and I could see that he half drew his knife.

"Well, brother," said he, "stand not here hungry in the highway when there is flesh and bread in the Rose yonder. Come on."

And with that he drew me along toward what was clearly a tavern door, outside which men were sitting on a couple of benches and drinking meditatively from curiously shaped earthen pots glazed green and yellow, some with quaint devices on them.

Chapter II

THE MAN FROM ESSEX

I entered the door and started at first with my old astonishment, with which I had woke up, so strange and beautiful did this interior seem to me, though it was but a pothouse parlor. A quaintly-carved sideboard held an array of bright pewter pots and dishes and wooden and earthen bowls; a stout oak table went up and down the room, and a carved oak chair stood by the chimney-corner, now filled by a very old man dim-eyed and white-bearded. That, except the rough stools and benches on which the company sat, was all the furniture. The walls were paneled roughly enough with oak boards to about six feet from the floor, and about three feet of plaster above that was wrought in a pattern of a rose stem running all round the room, freely and roughly done, but with (as it seemed to my unused eyes) wonderful skill and spirit. On the hood of the great chimney a huge rose was wrought in the plaster and brightly painted in its proper colors. There were a dozen or more of the men I had seen coming

along the street sitting there, some eating and all drinking; their cased bows leaned against the wall, their
quivers hung on pegs in the paneling, and in a corner
of the room I saw half-a-dozen billhooks that looked
made more for war than for hedge-shearing, with ashen
handles some seven foot long. Three or four children
were running about among the legs of the men, heeding them mighty little in their bold play, and the men
seemed little troubled by it, although they were talking
earnestly and seriously too. A well-made comely girl
leaned up against the chimney close to the gaffer's
chair, and seemed to be in waiting on the company:
she was clad in a close-fitting gown of bright blue cloth,
with a broad silver girdle daintily wrought, round her
loins, a rose wreath was on her head and her hair hung
down unbound; the gaffer grumbled a few words to
her from time to time, so that I judged he was her
grandfather.

The men all looked up as we came into the room,
my mate leading me by the hand, and he called out in
his rough, good-tempered voice, "Here, my masters, I
bring you tidings and a tale; give it meat and drink
that it may be strong and sweet."

"Whence are thy tidings, Will Green?" said one.

My mate grinned again with the pleasure of making
his joke once more in a bigger company: "It seemeth
from heaven, since this good old lad hath no master,"
said he.

"The more fool he to come here," said a thin man
with a grizzled beard, amidst the laughter that followed, "unless he had the choice given him between
hell and England."

"Nay," said I, "I come not from heaven, but from
Essex."

As I said the word a great shout sprang from all
mouths at once, as clear and sudden as a shot from a

gun. For I must tell you that I knew somehow, but I know not how, that the men of Essex were gathering to rise against the poll-groat bailiffs and the lords that would turn them all into villeins again, as their grandfathers had been. And the people was weak and the lords were poor; for many a mother's son had fallen in the war in France in the old king's time, and the Black Death had slain a many; so that the lords had bethought them: "We are growing poorer, and these upland-bred villeins are growing richer, and the guilds of craft are waxing in the towns, and soon what will there be left for us who cannot weave and will not dig? Good it were if we fell on all who are not guildsmen or men of free land, if we fell on soccage tenants and others, and brought both the law and the strong hand on them, and made them all villeins in deed as they are now in name; for now these rascals make more than their bellies need of bread, and their backs of homespun, and the overplus they keep to themselves; and we are more worthy of it than they. So let us get the collar on their necks again, and make their day's work longer and their bever-time shorter, as the good statute of the old king bade. And good it were if the Holy Church were to look to it (and the Lollards might help herein) that all these naughty and wearisome holidays were done away with; or that it should be unlawful for any man below the degree of a squire to keep the holy days of the church, except in the heart and the spirit only, and let the body labor meanwhile; for does not the Apostle say, 'If a man work not, neither should he eat'? And if such things were done, and such an estate of noble rich men and worthy poor men upholden forever, then would it be good times in England, and life were worth the living."

All this were the lords at work on, and such talk I knew was common not only among the lords themselves, but also among their sergeants and very serving-men. But the people would not abide it; therefore, as I said, in Essex they were on the point of rising, and word had gone how that at St. Albans they were well-nigh at blows with the Lord Abbot's soldiers; that north away at Norwich John Litster was wiping the woad from his arms, as who would have to stain them red again, but not with grain or madder; and that the valiant tiler of Dartford had smitten a poll-groat bailiff to death with his lath-rending axe for mishandling a young maid, his daughter; and that the men of Kent were on the move.

Now, knowing all this I was not astonished that they shouted at the thought of their fellows the men of Essex, but rather that they said little more about it; only Will Green saying quietly, "Well, the tidings shall be told when our fellowship is greater; fall-to now on the meat, brother, that we may the sooner have thy tale." As he spoke the blue-clad damsel bestirred herself and brought me a clean trencher — that is, a square piece of thin oak board scraped clean — and a pewter pot of liquor. So without more ado, and as one used to it, I drew my knife out of my girdle and cut myself what I would of the flesh and bread on the table. But Will Green mocked at me as I cut, and said, "Certes, brother, thou hast not been a lord's carver, though but for thy word thou mightest have been his reader. Hast thou seen Oxford, scholar?"

A vision of grey-roofed houses and a long winding street and the sound of many bells came over me at that word as I nodded "Yes" to him, my mouth full of salt pork and rye-bread; and then I lifted my pot and we made the clattering mugs kiss and I drank, and the fire of the good Kentish mead ran through my veins and deepened my dream of things past, present, and to come, as I said: "Now hearken a tale, since ye will have it so. For last autumn I was in Suffolk at the good town of Dunwich, and thither came the keels from Iceland, and on them were some men of Iceland, and many a tale they had on their tongues; and with these men I foregathered, for I am in sooth a gatherer of tales, and this that is now at my tongue's end is one of them."

So such a tale I told them, long familiar to me; but as I told it the words seemed to quicken and grow, so that I knew not the sound of my own voice, and they ran almost into rhyme and measure as I told it; and when I had done there was silence awhile, till one man spake, but not loudly:

"Yea, in that land was the summer short and the winter long; but men lived both summer and winter; and if the trees grew ill and the corn throve not, yet did the plant called man thrive and do well. God send us such men even here."

"Nay," said another, "such men have been and will be, and belike are not far from this same door even now."

"Yea," said a third, "hearken a stave of Robin Hood; maybe that shall hasten the coming of one I wot of." And he fell to singing in a clear voice, for he was a young man, and to a sweet wild melody, one of those ballads which in an incomplete and degraded form you have read perhaps. My heart rose high as I heard him, for it was concerning the struggle against tyranny for the freedom of life, how that the wildwood and the heath, despite of wind and weather, were better for a free man than the court and the cheaping-town; of the taking from the rich to give to the poor; of the life of a man doing his own will and not the will of another man commanding him for the commandment's sake. The men all listened eagerly, and at whiles took up as a refrain a couplet at the end of a stanza with their

strong and rough, but not unmusical voices. As they
sang, a picture of the wild-woods passed by me, as they
were indeed, no parklike dainty glades and lawns, but
rough and tangled thicket and bare waste and heath,
solemn under the morning sun, and dreary with the
rising of the evening wind and the drift of the night-
long rain.

When he had done, another began in something of
the same strain, but singing more of a song than a story
ballad; and thus much I remember of it:

The Sheriff is made a mighty lord,
Of goodly gold he hath enow,
And many a sergeant girt with sword;
But forth will we and bend the bow.
We shall bend the bow on the lily lea
Betwixt the thorn and the oaken tree.

With stone and lime is the burg wall built,
And pit and prison are stark and strong,
And many a true man there is spilt,
And many a right man doomed by wrong.
So forth shall we and bend the bow
And the king's writ never the road shall know.

Now yeomen walk ye warily,
And heed ye the houses where ye go,
For as fair and as fine as they may be,
Lest behind your heels the door clap to.
Fare forth with the bow to the lily lea
Betwixt the thorn and the oaken tree.

Now bills and bows I and out a-gate!
And turn about on the lily lea!
And though their company be great
The grey-goose wing shall set us free.

Now bent is the bow in the green abode
And the king's writ knoweth not the road.

So over the mead and over the hithe,
And away to the wild-wood wend we forth;
There dwell we yeomen bold and blithe
Where the Sheriff's word is naught of worth.
Bent is the bow on the lily lea
Betwixt the thorn and the oaken tree.

But here the song dropped suddenly, and one of the
men held up his hand as who would say, Hist! Then
through the open window came the sound of another
song, gradually swelling as though sung by men on the
march. This time the melody was a piece of the plain-
song of the church, familiar enough to me to bring
back to my mind the great arches of some cathedral in
France and the canons singing in the choir.

All leapt up and hurried to take their bows from wall
and corner; and some had bucklers withal, circles of
leather, boiled and then molded into shape and hardened: these were some two hand-breadths across, with
iron or brass bosses in the center. Will Green went to
the corner where the bills leaned against the wall and
handed them round to the first-comers as far as they
would go, and out we all went gravely and quietly into
the village street and the fair sunlight of the calm
afternoon, now beginning to turn towards evening.
None had said anything since we first heard the new-
come singing, save that as we went out of the door the
ballad-singer clapped me on the shoulder and said:

"Was it not sooth that I said, brother, that Robin
Hood should bring us John Ball?"

Chapter III

THEY MEET AT THE CROSS

*T*he street was pretty full of men by then we were out in it, and all faces turned toward the cross. The song still grew nearer and louder, and even as we looked we saw it turning the corner through the hedges of the orchards and closes, a good clump of men, more armed, as it would seem, than our villagers, as the low sun flashed back from many points of bright iron and steel. The words of the song could now be heard, and amidst them I could pick out Will Green's late challenge to me and my answer; but as I was bending all my mind to disentangle more words from the music, suddenly from the new white tower behind us clashed out the church bells, harsh and hurried at first, but presently falling into measured chime; and at the first sound of them a great shout went up from us and was echoed by the newcomers, "John Ball hath rung our bell!" Then we pressed on, and presently we were all mingled together at the cross.

Will Green had good-naturedly thrust and pulled me

forward, so that I found myself standing on the lowest step of the cross, his seventy-two inches of man on one side of me. He chuckled while I panted, and said:

"There's for thee a good hearing and seeing stead, old lad. Thou art tall across thy belly and not otherwise, and thy wind, belike, is none of the best, and but for me thou wouldst have been amidst the thickest of the throng, and have heard words muffled by Kentish bellies and seen little but swinky woolen elbows and greasy plates and jacks. Look no more on the ground, as though thou sawest a hare, but let thine eyes and thine ears be busy to gather tidings to bear back to Essex — or heaven!"

I grinned good-fellowship at him but said nothing, for in truth my eyes and ears were as busy as he would have them to be. A buzz of general talk went up from the throng amidst the regular cadence of the bells, which now seemed far away and as it were that they were not swayed by hands, but were living creatures making that noise of their own wills.

I looked around and saw that the newcomers mingled with us must have been a regular armed band; all had bucklers slung at their backs, few lacked a sword at the side. Some had bows, some "staves" — that is, bills, pole-axes, or pikes. Moreover, unlike our villagers, they had defensive arms. Most had steel-caps on their heads, and some had body armor, generally a "jack," or coat into which pieces of iron or horn were quilted; some had also steel or steel-and-leather arm or thigh pieces. There were a few mounted men among them, their horses being big-boned hammer-headed beasts, that looked as if they had been taken from plow or wagon, but their riders were well armed with steel armor on their heads, legs, and arms. Amongst the horsemen I noted the man that had ridden past me when I first awoke; but he seemed to be a prisoner, as he had a woolen hood on his head instead of his helmet, and carried neither bill, sword, nor dagger. He seemed by no means ill-at-ease, however, but was laughing and talking with the men who stood near him.

Above the heads of the crowd, and now slowly working towards the cross, was a banner on a high-raised cross-pole, a picture of a man and woman half-clad in skins of beasts seen against a background of green trees, the man holding a spade and the woman a distaff and spindle rudely done enough, but yet with a certain spirit and much meaning; and underneath this symbol of the early world and man's first contest with nature were the written words:

When Adam delved and Eve span
Who was then the gentleman?

The banner came on and through the crowd, which at last opened where we stood for its passage, and the banner-bearer turned and faced the throng and stood on the first step of the cross beside me.

A man followed him, clad in a long dark-brown gown of coarse woolen, girt with a cord, to which hung a "pair of beads" (or rosary, as we should call it today) and a book in a bag. The man was tall and big-boned, a ring of dark hair surrounded his priest's tonsure; his nose was big but clear cut and with wide nostrils; his shaven face showed a longish upper lip and a big but blunt chin; his mouth was big and the lips closed firmly; a face not very noteworthy but for his grey eyes well opened and wide apart, at whiles lighting up his whole face with a kindly smile, at whiles set and stern, at whiles resting in that look as if they were gazing at something a long way off, which is the wont of the eyes of the poet or enthusiast.

He went slowly up the steps of the cross and stood

at the top with one hand laid on the shaft, and shout upon shout broke forth from the throng. When the shouting died away into a silence of the human voices, the bells were still quietly chiming with that faraway voice of theirs, and the long-winged dusky swifts, by no means scared by the concourse, swung round about the cross with their wild squeals; and the man stood still for a little, eyeing the throng, or rather looking first at one and then another man in it, as though he were trying to think what such an one was thinking of, or what he were fit for. Sometimes he caught the eye of one or other, and then that kindly smile spread over his face, but faded off it into the sternness and sadness of a man who has heavy and great thoughts hanging about him.

But when John Ball first mounted the steps of the cross a lad at someone's bidding had run off to stop the ringers, and so presently the voice of the bells fell dead, leaving on men's minds that sense of blankness or even disappointment which is always caused by the sudden stopping of a sound one has got used to and found pleasant. But a great expectation had fallen by now on all that throng, and no word was spoken even in a whisper, and all men's hearts and eyes were fixed upon the dark figure standing straight up now by the tall white shaft of the cross, his hands stretched out before him, one palm laid upon the other. And for me, as I made ready to hearken, I felt a joy in my soul that I had never yet felt.

Chapter IV

THE VOICE OF JOHN BALL

*S*o now I heard John Ball; how he lifted up his voice and said:

"Ho, all ye good people! I am a priest of God, and in my day's work it cometh that I should tell you what ye should do, and what ye should forbear doing, and to that end I am come hither: yet first, if I myself have wronged any man here, let him say wherein my wrong-doing lieth, that I may ask his pardon and his pity."

A great hum of good-will ran through the crowd as he spoke; then he smiled as in a kind of pride, and again he spoke:

"Wherefore did ye take me out of the archbishop's prison but three days agone, when ye lighted the archbishop's house for the candle of Canterbury, but that I might speak to you and pray you: therefore I will not keep silence, whether I have done ill, or whether I have done well. And herein, good fellows and my very brethren, I would have you to follow me; and if there be such here, as I know full well there be some, and may be a good many, who have been robbers of their neighbors ('And who is my neighbor?' quoth the rich man), or lechers, or despiteful haters, or talebearers, or fawners on rich men for the hurt of the poor (and that is the worst of all) — Ah, my poor brethren who have gone astray, I say not to you, go home and repent lest you mar our great deeds, but rather come afield and there repent. Many a day have ye been fools, but hearken unto me and I shall make you wise above the wisdom of the earth; and if ye die in your wisdom, as God wot ye well may, since the fields ye wend to bear swords for daisies, and spears for bents, then shall ye be, though men call you dead, a part and parcel of the living wisdom of all things, very stones of the pillars that uphold the joyful earth.

"Forsooth, ye have heard it said that ye shall do well in this world that in the world to come ye may live happily forever; do ye well then, and have your reward both on earth and in heaven; for I say to you that earth and heaven are not two but one; and this one is that which ye know, and are each one of you a part of, to wit, the Holy Church, and in each one of you dwelleth the life of the Church, unless ye slay it. Forsooth, brethren, will ye murder the Church anyone of you, and go forth a wandering man and lonely, even as Cain did who slew his brother? Ah, my brothers, what an evil doom is this, to be an outcast from the Church, to have none to love you and to speak with you, to be without fellowship! Forsooth, brothers, fellowship is heaven, and lack of fellowship is hell: fellowship is life, and lack of fellowship is death: and the deeds that ye do upon the earth, it is for fellowship's sake that ye do them, and the life that is in it, that shall live on and on forever, and each one of you part of it, while many a man's life upon the earth from the earth shall wane.

"Therefore, I bid you not dwell in hell but in heaven,

or while ye must, upon earth, which is a part of heaven, and forsooth no foul part.

"Forsooth, he that waketh in hell and feeleth his heart fail him, shall have memory of the merry days of earth, and how that when his heart failed him there, he cried on his fellow, were it his wife or his son or his brother or his gossip or his brother sworn in arms, and how that his fellow heard him and came and they mourned together under the sun, till again they laughed together and were but half sorry between them. This shall he think on in hell, and cry on his fellow to help him, and shall find that therein is no help because there is no fellowship, but every man for himself. Therefore, I tell you that the proud, despiteous rich man, though he knoweth it not, is in hell already, because he hath no fellow; and he that hath so hardy a heart that in sorrow he thinketh of fellowship, his sorrow is soon but a story of sorrow — a little change in the life that knows not ill."

He left off for a little; and indeed for some time his voice had fallen, but it was so clear and the summer evening so soft and still, and the silence of the folk so complete, that every word told. His eyes fell down to the crowd as he stopped speaking, since for some little while they had been looking far away into the blue distance of summer; and the kind eyes of the man had a curious sight before him in that crowd, for amongst them were many who by this time were not dry-eyed, and some wept outright in spite of their black beards, while all had that look as if they were ashamed of themselves, and did not want others to see how deeply they were moved, after the fashion of their race when they are strongly stirred. I looked at Will Green beside me: his right hand clutched his bow so tight, that the knuckles whitened; he was staring straight before him, and the tears were running out of his eyes and down his big nose as though without his will, for his face was stolid and unmoved all the time till he caught my eye, and then he screwed up the strangest face, of scowling brow, weeping eyes, and smiling mouth, while he dealt me a sounding thump in the ribs with his left elbow, which, though it would have knocked me down but for the crowd, I took as an esquire does the accolade which makes a knight of him.

But while I pondered all these things, and how men fight and lose the battle, and the thing that they fought for comes about in spite of their defeat, and when it comes turns out not to be what they meant, and other men have to fight for what they meant under another name — while I pondered all this, John Ball began to speak again in the same soft and dear voice with which he had left off.

"Good fellows, it was your fellowship and your kindness that took me out of the archbishop's prison three days agone, though God wot ye had naught to gain by it save outlawry and the gallows; yet lacked I not your fellowship before ye drew near me in the body, and when between me and Canterbury street was yet a strong wall, and the turnkeys and sergeants and bailiffs.

"For hearken, my friends and helpers; many days ago, when April was yet young, I lay there, and the heart that I had strung up to bear all things because of the fellowship of men and the blessed saints and the angels and those that are, and those that are to be, this heart, that I had strung up like a strong bow, fell into feebleness, so that I lay there a-longing for the green fields and the white-thorn bushes and the lark singing over the corn, and the talk of good fellows round the ale-house bench, and the babble of the little children, and the team on the road and the beasts afield, and all the life of earth; and I alone all the while, near my foes and afar from my friends, mocked and flouted and starved with cold and hunger; and so weak was my heart that though I longed for all these things yet I saw them not, nor knew them but as names; and I longed so sore to be gone that I chided myself that I had once done well; and I said to myself:

"Forsooth, hadst thou kept thy tongue between thy teeth thou mightest have been something, if it had been but a parson of a town, and comfortable to many a poor man; and then mightest thou have clad here and there the naked back, and filled the empty belly, and holpen many, and men would have spoken well of thee, and of thyself thou hadst thought well; and all this hast thou lost for lack of a word here and there to some great man, and a little winking of the eyes amidst murder and wrong and unruth; and now thou art naught and helpless, and the hemp for thee is sown and grown and heckled and spun, and lo there, the rope for thy gallows tree! — all for naught, for naught.

"Forsooth, my friends, thus I thought and sorrowed in my feebleness that I had not been a traitor to the Fellowship of the Church, for e'en so evil was my foolish imagination.

"Yet, forsooth, as I fell a-pondering over all the comfort and help that I might have been and that I might have had, if I had been but a little of a trembling cur to creep and crawl before abbot and bishop and baron and bailiff, came the thought over me of the evil of the world wherewith I, John Ball, the rascal hedge-priest, had fought and striven in the Fellowship of the saints in heaven and poor men upon earth.

"Yea, forsooth, once again I saw as of old, the great treading down the little, and the strong beating down the weak, and cruel men fearing not, and kind men daring not, and wise men caring not; and the saints in heaven forbearing and yet bidding me not to forbear;

forsooth, I knew once more that he who doeth well in fellowship, and because of fellowship, shall not fail though he seem to fail today, but in days hereafter shall he and his work yet be alive, and men be holpen by them to strive again and yet again; and yet indeed even that was little, since, forsooth, to strive was my pleasure and my life.

"So I became a man once more, and I rose up to my feet and went up and down my prison what I could for my hopples, and into my mouth came words of good cheer, even such as we today have sung, and stoutly I sang them, even as we now have sung them; and then did I rest me, and once more thought of those pleasant fields where I would be, and all the life of man and beast about them, and I said to myself that I should see them once more before I died, if but once it were.

"Forsooth, this was strange, that whereas before I longed for them and yet saw them not, now that my longing was slaked my vision was cleared, and I saw them as though the prison walls opened to me and I was out of Canterbury street and amidst the green meadows of April; and therewithal along with me folk that I have known and who are dead, and folk that are living; yea, and all those of the Fellowship on earth and in heaven; yea, and all that are here this day. Overlong were the tale to tell of them, and of the time that is gone.

"So thenceforward I wore through the days with no such faint heart, until one day the prison opened verily and in the daylight, and there were ye, my fellows, in the door — your faces glad, your hearts light with hope, and your hands heavy with wrath; then I saw and understood what was to do. Now, therefore, do ye understand it!"

His voice was changed, and grew louder than loud now, as he cast his hands abroad towards that company with those last words of his; and I could feel that all shame and fear was falling from those men, and that mere fiery manhood was shining through their wonted English shamefast stubbornness, and that they were moved indeed and saw the road before them. Yet no man spoke, rather the silence of the menfolk deepened, as the sun's rays grew more level and more golden, and the swifts wheeled about shriller and louder than before.

Then again John Ball spoke and said, "In good sooth, I deem ye wot no worse than I do what is to do — and first that somewhat we shall do — since it is for him that is lonely or in prison to dream of fellowship, but for him that is of a fellowship to do and not to dream.

"And next, ye know who is the foeman, and that is the proud man, the oppressor, who scorneth fellowship, and himself is a world to himself and needeth no helper nor helpeth any, but, heeding no law, layeth law on other men because he is rich; and surely everyone that is rich is such an one, nor may be other.

"Forsooth, in the belly of every rich man dwelleth a devil of hell, and when the man would give his goods to the poor, the devil within him gainsayeth it, and saith, 'Wilt thou then be of the poor, and suffer cold and hunger and mocking as they suffer, then give thou thy goods to them, and keep them not.' And when he would be compassionate, again saith the devil to him, 'If thou heed these losels and turn on them a face like to their faces, and deem of them as men, then shall they scorn thee, and evil shall come of it, and even one day they shall fall on thee to slay thee when they have learned that thou art but as they be.'

"Ah, woe worth the while! too oft he sayeth sooth, as the wont of the devil is, that lies may be born of the barren truth; and sooth it is that the poor deemeth the rich to be other than he, and meet to be his master, as though, forsooth, the poor were come of Adam, and the rich of him that made Adam, that is God; and thus the poor man oppresseth the poor man, because he feareth the oppressor. Naught such are ye, my brethren; or else why are ye gathered here in harness to bid all bear witness of you that ye are the sons of one man and one mother, begotten of the earth?"

As he said the words there came a stir among the weapons of the throng, and they pressed closer round the cross, yet withheld the shout as yet which seemed gathering in their bosoms.

And again he said:

"Forsooth, too many rich men there are in this realm; and yet if there were but one, there would be one too many, for all should be his thralls. Hearken, then, ye men of Kent. For overlong belike have I held you with words; but the love of you constrained me, and the joy that a man hath to babble to his friends and his fellows whom he hath not seen for a long season.

"Now, hearken, I bid you: To the rich men that eat up a realm there cometh a time when they whom they eat up, that is the poor, seem poorer than of wont, and their complaint goeth up louder to the heavens; yet it is no riddle to say that oft at such times the fellowship of the poor is waxing stronger, else would no man have heard his cry. Also at such times is the rich man become fearful, and so waxeth in cruelty, and of that cruelty do people misdeem that it is power and might waxing. Forsooth, ye are stronger than your fathers, because ye are more grieved than they, and ye should have been less grieved than they had ye been horses and swine; and then, forsooth, would ye have been stronger to bear; but ye, ye are not strong to bear, but to do.

"And wot ye why we are come to you this fair eve of holiday? and wot ye why I have been telling of fellowship to you? Yea, forsooth, I deem ye wot well, that it is for this cause, that ye might bethink you of your fellowship with the men of Essex."

His last word let loose the shout that had been long on all men's lips, and great and fierce it was as it rang shattering through the quiet upland village. But John Ball held up his hand, and the shout was one and no more.

Then he spoke again:

"Men of Kent, I wot well that ye are not so hard bested as those of other shires, by the token of the day when behind the screen of leafy boughs ye met Duke William with bill and bow as he wended Londonward from that woeful field of Senlac; but I have told of fellowship, and ye have hearkened and understood what the Holy Church is, whereby ye know that ye are fellows of the saints in heaven and the poor men of Essex; and as one day the saints shall call you to the heavenly feast, so now do the poor men call you to the battle.

"Men of Kent, ye dwell fairly here, and your houses are framed of stout oak beams, and your own lands ye till; unless some accursed lawyer with his false lying sheepskin and forged custom of the Devil's Manor hath stolen it from you; but in Essex slaves they be and villeins, and worse they shall be, and the lords swear that ere a year be over ox and horse shall go free in Essex, and man and woman shall draw the team and the plow; and north away in the east countries dwell men in poor halls of wattled reeds and mud, and the northeast wind from off the fen whistles through them; and poor they be to the letter; and there him whom the lord spareth, the bailiff squeezeth, and him whom the bailiff forgetteth, the Easterling Chapman sheareth; yet be these stout men and valiant, and your very brethren.

"And yet if there be any man here so base as to think that a small matter, let him look to it that if these necks abide under the yoke, Kent shall sweat for it ere it be long; and ye shall lose acre and close and woodland, and be servants in your own houses, and your sons shall be the lords' lads, and your daughters their le-mans, and ye shall buy a bold word with many stripes, and an honest deed with a leap from the gallows tree.

"Bethink ye, too, that ye have no longer to deal with Duke William, who, if he were a thief and a cruel lord, was yet a prudent man and a wise warrior; but cruel are these, and headstrong, yea, thieves and fools in one — and ye shall lay their heads in the dust."

A shout would have arisen again, but his eager voice rising higher yet, restrained it as he said:

"And how shall it be then when these are gone? What else shall ye lack when ye lack masters? Ye shall not lack for the fields ye have tilled, nor the houses ye have built, nor the cloth ye have woven; all these shall be yours, and whatso ye will of all that the earth beareth; then shall no man mow the deep grass for another, while his own kine lack cow-meat; and he that soweth shall reap, and the reaper shall eat in fellowship the harvest that in fellowship he hath won; and he that buildeth a house shall dwell in it with those that he biddeth of his free will; and the tithe barn shall garner the wheat for all men to eat of when the seasons are untoward, and the rain-drift hideth the sheaves in August; and all shall be without money and without price. Faithfully and merrily then shall all men keep the holidays of the Church in peace of body and joy of heart. And man shall help man, and the saints in heaven shall be glad, because men no more fear each other; and the churl shall be ashamed, and shall hide his churlishness till it be gone, and he be no more a churl; and fellowship shall be established in heaven and on the earth."

Chapter V

THEY HEAR TIDINGS OF BATTLE AND MAKE THEM READY

*H*e left off as one who had yet something else to say; and, indeed, I thought he would give us some word as to the trysting-place, and whither the army was to go from it; because it was now clear to me that this gathering was but a band of an army. But much happened before John Ball spoke again from the cross, and it was on this wise.

When there was silence after the last shout that the crowd had raised a while ago, I thought I heard a thin sharp noise far away, somewhat to the north of the cross, which I took rather for the sound of a trumpet or horn, than for the voice of a man or any beast. Will Green also seemed to have heard it, for he turned his head sharply and then back again, and looked keenly into the crowd as though seeking to catch someone's eye. There was a very tall man standing by the prisoner on the horse near the outskirts of the crowd, and holding his bridle. This man, who was well-armed, I saw look up and say something to the prisoner, who stooped down and seemed to whisper him in turn. The tall man nodded his head and the prisoner got off his horse, which was a cleaner-limbed, better-built beast than the others belonging to the band, and the tall man quietly led him a little way from the crowd, mounted him, and rode off northward at a smart pace.

Will Green looked on sharply at all this, and when the man rode off, smiled as one who is content, and deems that all is going well, and settled himself down again to listen to the priest.

But now when John Ball had ceased speaking, and after another shout, and a hum of excited pleasure and hope that followed it, there was silence again, and as the priest addressed himself to speaking once more, he paused and turned his head towards the wind, as if he heard something, which certainly I heard, and belike everyone in the throng, though it was not overloud, far as sounds carry in clear quiet evenings. It was the thump-a-thump of a horse drawing near at a hand-gallop along the grassy upland road; and I knew well it was the tall man coming back with tidings, the purport of which I could well guess.

I looked up at Will Green's face. He was smiling as one pleased, and said softly as he nodded to me, "Yea, shall we see the grey-goose fly this eve?"

But John Ball said in a great voice from the cross, "Hear ye the tidings on the way, fellows! Hold ye together and look to your gear; yet hurry not, for no great matter shall this be. I wot well there is little force between Canterbury and Kingston, for the lords are looking north of Thames toward Wat Tyler and his men. Yet well it is, well it is!"

The crowd opened and spread out a little, and the

men moved about in it, some tightening a girdle, some getting their side arms more within reach of their right hands, and those who had bows stringing them.

Will Green set hand and foot to the great shapely piece of polished red yew, with its shining horn tips, which he carried, and bent it with no seeming effort; then he reached out his hand over his shoulder and drew out a long arrow, smooth, white, beautifully balanced, with a barbed iron head at one end, a horn nock and three strong goose feathers at the other. He held it loosely between the finger and thumb of his right hand, and there he stood with a thoughtful look on his face, and in his hands one of the most terrible weapons which a strong man has ever carried, the English long-bow and cloth-yard shaft.

But all this while the sound of the horse's hoofs was growing nearer, and presently from the corner of the road amidst the orchards broke out our long friend, his face red in the sun near sinking now. He waved his right hand as he came in sight of us, and sang out, "Bills and bows! bills and bows!" and the whole throng turned towards him and raised a great shout.

He reined up at the edge of the throng, and spoke in a loud voice, so that all might hear him:

"Fellows, these are the tidings; even while our priest was speaking we heard a horn blow far off; so I bade the sergeant we have taken, and who is now our fellow-in-arms, to tell me where away it was that there would be folk a-gathering, and what they were; and he did me to wit that mayhappen Sir John Newton was stirring from Rochester Castle; or, maybe, it was the sheriff and Rafe Hopton with him; so I rode off what I might towards Hartlip, and I rode warily, and that was well, for as I came through a little wood between Hartlip and Guildstead, I saw beyond it a gleam of steel, and lo in the field there a company, and a pennon of Rafe

Hopton's arms, and that is blue and thereon three
silver fish: and a pennon of the sheriff's arms, and that
is a green tree; and withal another pennon of three red
kine, and whose they be I know not. Probably one of
the Calverlys, a Cheshire family, one of whom was a
noted captain in the French wars.

"There tied I my horse in the middle of the wood,
and myself I crept along the dyke to see more and to
hear somewhat; and no talk I heard to tell of save at
whiles a big knight talking to five or six others, and
saying somewhat, wherein came the words London and
Nicholas Bramber, and King Richard; but I saw that
of men-at-arms and sergeants there might be a hundred,
and of bows not many, but of those outland arbalests
maybe a fifty; and so, what with one and another of
servants and tipstaves and lads, some three hundred,
well armed, and the men-at-arms of the best. Forsooth,
my masters, there had I been but a minute, ere the big
knight broke off his talk, and cried out to the music
to blow up, 'And let us go look on these villeins,' said
he; and withal the men began to gather in a due and
ordered company, and their faces turned hitherward;
forsooth, I got to my horse, and led him out of the
wood on the other side, and so to saddle and away
along the green roads; neither was I seen or chased. So
look ye to it, my masters, for these men will be coming
to speak with us; nor is there need for haste, but rather
for good speed; for in some twenty or thirty minutes
will be more tidings to hand."

By this time one of our best-armed men had got
through the throng and was standing on the cross
beside John Ball. When the long man had done, there
was confused noise of talk for a while, and the throng
spread itself out more and more, but not in a disorderly
manner; the bowmen drawing together toward the
outside, and the billmen forming behind them. Will

Green was still standing beside me and had hold of my arm, as though he knew both where he and I were to go.

"Fellows," quoth the captain from the cross, "belike this stour shall not live to be older than the day, if ye get not into a plump together for their arbalestiers to shoot bolts into, and their men-at-arms to thrust spears into. Get you to the edge of the crofts and spread out there six feet between man and man, and shoot, ye bowmen, from the hedges, and ye with the staves keep your heads below the level of the hedges, or else for all they be thick a bolt may win its way in."

He grinned as he said this, and there was laughter enough in the throng to have done honor to a better joke.

Then he sung out, "Hob Wright, Rafe Wood, John Pargetter, and thou Will Green, bestir ye and marshal the bowshot; and thou Nicholas Woodyer shall be under me Jack Straw in ordering of the staves. Gregory Tailor and John Clerk, fair and fine are ye clad in the arms of the Canterbury bailiffs; ye shall shine from afar; go ye with the banner into the highway, and the bows on either side shall ward you; yet jump, lads, and over the hedge with you when the bolts begin to fly your way! Take heed, good fellows all, that our business is to bestride the highway, and not let them get in on our flank the while; so half to the right, half to the left of the highway. Shoot straight and strong, and waste no breath with noise; let the loose of the bowstring cry for you! and look you! think it no loss of manhood to cover your bodies with tree and bush; for one of us who know is worth a hundred of those proud fools. To it, lads, and let them see what the grey goose bears between his wings! Abide us here, brother John Ball, and pray for us if thou wilt; but for me, if God will not do for Jack Straw what Jack Straw would do for

God were he in like case, I can see no help for it."

"Yea, forsooth," said the priest, "here will I abide you my fellows if ye come back; or if ye come not back, here will I abide the foe. Depart, and the blessing of the Fellowship be with you."

Down then leapt Jack Straw from the cross, and the whole throng set off without noise or hurry, soberly and steadily in outward seeming. Will Green led me by the hand as if I were a boy, yet nothing he said, being forsooth intent on his charge. We were some four hundred men in all; but I said to myself that without some advantage of the ground we were lost men before the men-at-arms that long Gregory Tailor had told us of; for I had not seen as yet the yard-long shaft at its work.

We and somewhat more than half of our band turned into the orchards on the left of the road, through which the level rays of the low sun shone brightly. The others took up their position on the right side of it. We kept pretty near to the road till we had got through all the closes save the last, where we were brought up by a hedge and a dyke, beyond which lay a wide-open nearly treeless space, not of tillage, as at the other side of the place, but of pasture, the common grazing ground of the township. A little stream wound about through the ground, with a few willows here and there; there was only a thread of water in it in this hot summer tide, but its course could easily be traced by the deep blue-green of the rushes that grew plenteously in the bed. Geese were lazily wandering about and near this brook, and a herd of cows, accompanied by the town bull, were feeding on quietly, their heads all turned one way; while half a dozen calves marched close together side by side like a plump of soldiers, their tails swinging in a kind of measure to keep off the flies, of which there was great plenty. Three or four lads and girls were sauntering about, heeding or not heeding the cattle. They looked up toward us as we crowded into the last close, and slowly loitered off toward the village. Nothing looked like battle; yet battle sounded in the air; for now we heard the beat of the horse-hoofs of the men-at-arms coming on towards us like the rolling of distant thunder, and growing louder and louder every minute; we were none too soon in turning to face them. Jack Straw was on our side of the road, and with a few gestures and a word or two he got his men into their places. Six archers lined the hedge along the road where the banner of Adam and Eve, rising above the grey leaves of the apple trees, challenged the newcomers; and of the billmen also he kept a good few ready to guard the road in case the enemy should try to rush it with the horsemen. The road, not being a Roman one, was, you must remember, little like the firm smooth country roads that you are used to; it was a mere track between the hedges and fields, partly grass-grown, and cut up by the deep-sunk ruts hardened by the drought of summer. There was a stack of fagot and small wood on the other side, and our men threw themselves upon it and set to work to stake the road across for a rough defense against the horsemen.

What befell more on the road itself I had not much time to note, for our bowmen spread themselves out along the hedge that looked into the pasture-field, leaving some six feet between man and man; the rest of the billmen went along with the bowmen, and halted in clumps of some half-dozen along their line, holding themselves ready to help the bowmen if the enemy should run up under their shafts, or to run on to lengthen the line in case they should try to break in on our flank. The hedge in front of us was of quick. It had been strongly plashed in the past February, and was stiff and stout. It stood on a low bank; moreover, the level of the orchard was some thirty inches higher than that of the field. and the ditch some two foot deeper than the face of the field. The field went winding round to beyond the church, making a quarter of a circle about the village, and at the western end of it were the butts whence the folk were coming from shooting when I first came into the village street.

Altogether, to me who knew nothing of war the place seemed defensible enough. I have said that the road down which Long Gregory came with his tidings went north; and that was its general direction; but its first reach was nearly east, so that the low sun was not in the eyes of any of us, and where Will Green took his stand, and I with him, it was nearly at our backs.

Chapter VI

THE BATTLE AT THE TOWNSHIP'S END

Our men had got into their places leisurely and coolly enough, and with no lack of jesting and laughter. As we went along the hedge by the road, the leaders tore off leafy twigs from the low oak bushes therein, and set them for a rallying sign in their hats and headpieces, and two or three of them had horns for blowing.

Will Green, when he got into his place, which was thirty yards from where Jack Straw and the billmen stood in the corner of the two hedges, the road hedge and the hedge between the close and field, looked to right and left of him a moment, then turned to the man on the left and said:

"Look you, mate, when you hear our horns blow ask no more questions, but shoot straight and strong at whatso cometh towards us, till ye hear more tidings from Jack Straw or from me. Pass that word onward."

Then he looked at me and said:

"Now, lad from Essex, thou hadst best sit down out of the way at once: forsooth I wot not why I brought thee hither. Wilt thou not back to the cross, for thou art little of a fighting-man?"

"Nay," said I, "I would see the play. What shall come of it?"

"Little," said he; "we shall slay a horse or twain maybe. I will tell thee, since thou hast not seen a fight belike, as I have seen some, that these men-at-arms cannot run fast either to the play or from it, if they be a-foot; and if they come on a-horseback, what shall hinder me to put a shaft into the poor beast? But down with thee on the daisies, for some shot there will be first."

As he spoke he was pulling off his belts and other gear, and his coat, which done, he laid his quiver on the ground, girt him again, did his axe and buckler on to his girdle, and hung up his other attire on the nearest tree behind us. Then he opened his quiver and took out of it some two dozen of arrows, which he stuck in the ground beside him ready to his hand. Most of the bowmen within sight were doing the like.

As I glanced toward the houses I saw three or four bright figures moving through the orchards, and presently noted that they were women, all clad more or less like the girl in the Rose, except that two of them wore white coifs on their heads. Their errand there was clear, for each carried a bundle of arrows under her arm.

One of them came straight up to Will Green, and I could see at once that she was his daughter. She was tall and strongly made, with black hair like her father, somewhat comely, though no great beauty; but as they met, her eyes smiled even more than her mouth, and made her face look very sweet and kind, and the smile was answered back in a way so quaintly like to her father's face, that I too smiled for goodwill and pleasure.

"Well, well, lass," said he, "dost thou think that here is Crecy field toward, that ye bring all this artillery? Turn back, my girl, and set the pot on the fire; for that shall we need when we come home, I and this ballad-maker here."

"Nay," she said, nodding kindly at me, "if this is to be no Crecy, then may I stop to see, as well as the ballad-maker, since he hath neither sword nor staff?"

"Sweetling," he said, "get thee home in haste. This play is but little, yet mightest thou be hurt in it; and trust me the time may come, sweetheart, when even thou and such as thou shalt hold a sword or a staff. Ere the moon throws a shadow we shall be back."

She turned away lingering, not without tears on her face, laid the sheaf of arrows at the foot of the tree, and hastened off through the orchard. I was going to say something, when Will Green held up his hand as who would bid us hearken. The noise of the horse-hoofs, after growing nearer and nearer, had ceased suddenly, and a confused murmur of voices had taken the place of it.

"Get thee down, and take cover, old lad," said Will Green; "the dance will soon begin, and ye shall hear the music presently."

Sure enough as I slipped down by the hedge close to which I had been standing, I heard the harsh twang of the bow-strings, one, two, three, almost together, from the road, and even the whew of the shafts, though that was drowned in a moment by a confused but loud and threatening shout from the other side, and again the bowstrings clanged, and this time a far-off clash of arms followed, and therewithal that cry of a strong man that comes without his will, and is so different from his wonted voice that one has a guess thereby of the change that death is. Then for a while was almost silence; nor did our horns blow up, though some half-dozen of the billmen had leapt into the road when the bows first shot. But presently came a great blare of trumpets and horns from the other side, and therewith as it were a river of steel and bright coats poured into the field before us, and still their horns blew as they spread out toward the left of our line; the cattle in the pasture-field, heretofore feeding quietly, seemed frightened silly by the sudden noise, and ran about tail in air and lowing loudly; the old bull with his head a little lowered, and his stubborn legs planted firmly, growling threateningly; while the geese about the brook waddled away gobbling and squeaking; all which seemed so strange to us along with the threat of sudden death that rang out from the bright array over against us, that we laughed outright, the most of us, and Will Green put down his head in mockery of the bull and grunted like him, whereat we laughed yet more. He turned round to me as he nocked his arrow, and said:

"I would they were just fifty paces nigher, and they move not. Ho! Jack Straw, shall we shoot?"

For the latter-named was nigh us now; he shook his head and said nothing as he stood looking at the enemy's line.

"Fear not but they are the right folk, Jack," quoth Will Green.

"Yea, yea," said he, "but abide awhile; they could make naught of the highway, and two of their sergeants had a message from the grey-goose feather. Abide, for they have not crossed the road to our right hand, and belike have not seen our fellows on the other side, who are now for a bushment to them."

I looked hard at the man. He was a tall, wiry, and broad-shouldered fellow, clad in a handsome armor of bright steel that certainly had not been made for a yeoman, but over it he had a common linen smock-frock or gabardine, like our field workmen wear now or used to wear, and in his helmet he carried instead of a feather a wisp of wheaten straw. He bore a heavy axe in his hand besides the sword he was girt with, and round his neck hung a great horn for blowing. I should say that I knew that there were at least three "Jack Straws" among the fellowship of the discontented, one of whom was over in Essex.

As we waited there, every bowman with his shaft nocked on the string, there was a movement in the line opposite, and presently came from it a little knot of three men, the middle one on horseback, the other two armed with long-handled glaives; all three well muffled up in armor. As they came nearer I could see that the horseman had a tabard over his armor, gaily embroidered with a green tree on a gold ground, and in his hand a trumpet.

"They are come to summon us. Wilt thou that he speak, Jack?" said Will Green.

"Nay," said the other; "yet shall he have warning first. Shoot when my horn blows!"

And therewith he came up to the hedge, climbed over, slowly because of his armor, and stood some dozen yards out in the field. The man on horseback put his trumpet to his mouth and blew a long blast, and then took a scroll into his hand and made as if he were going to read; but Jack Straw lifted up his voice and cried out:

"Do it not, or thou art but dead! We will have no accursed lawyers and their sheep-skins here! Go back to those that sent thee —"

But the man broke in in a loud harsh voice:

"Ho! YE PEOPLE! what will ye gathering in arms?"

Then cried Jack Straw:

"Sir Fool, hold your peace till ye have heard me, or

else we shoot at once. Go back to those that sent thee, and tell them that we free men of Kent are on the way to London to speak with King Richard, and to tell him that which he wots not; to wit, that there is a certain sort of fools and traitors to the realm who would put collars on our necks and make beasts of us, and that it is his right and his devoir to do as he swore when he was crowned and anointed at Westminster on the Stone of Doom, and gainsay these thieves and traitors; and if he be too weak, then shall we help him; and if he will not be king, then shall we have one who will be, and that is the King's Son of Heaven. Now, therefore, if any withstand us on our lawful errand as we go to speak with our own king and lord, let him look to it. Bear back this word to them that sent thee. But for thee, hearken, thou bastard of an inky sheep-skin! get thee gone and tarry not; three times shall I lift up my hand, and the third time look to thyself, for then shalt thou hear the loose of our bowstrings, and after that naught else till thou hearest the devil bidding thee welcome to hell!"

Our fellows shouted, but the summoner began again, yet in a quavering voice:

"Ho! YE PEOPLE! what will ye gathering in arms? Wot ye not that ye are doing or shall do great harm, loss, and hurt to the king's lieges —"

He stopped; Jack Straw's hand was lowered for the second time. He looked to his men right and left, and then turned rein and turned tail, and scuttled back to the main body at his swiftest. Huge laughter rattled out all along our line as Jack Straw climbed back into the orchard grinning also.

Then we noted more movement in the enemy's line. They were spreading the archers and arbalestiers to our left, and the men-at-arms and others also spread some, what under the three pennons of which Long Gregory had told us, and which were plain enough to us in the dear evening. Presently the moving line faced us, and the archers set off at a smart pace toward us, the men-at-arms holding back a little behind them. I knew now that they had been within bowshot all along, but our men were loath to shoot before their first shots would tell, like those half-dozen in the road when, as they told me afterwards, a plump of their men-at-arms had made a show of falling on.

But now as soon as those men began to move on us directly in face, Jack Straw put his horn to his lips and blew a loud rough blast that was echoed by five or six others along the orchard hedge. Every man had his shaft nocked on the string; I watched them, and Will Green specially; he and his bow and its string seemed all of a piece, so easily by seeming did he draw the nock of the arrow to his ear. A moment, as he took his aim, and then — O then did I under stand the meaning of the awe with which the ancient poet speaks of the loose of the god Apollo's bow; for terrible indeed was the mingled sound of the twanging bowstring and the whirring shaft so close to me.

I was now on my knees right in front of Will and saw all clearly; the arbalestiers (for no long-bow men were over against our stead) had all of them bright headpieces, and stout body-armor of boiled leather with metal studs, and as they came towards us, I could see over their shoulders great wooden shields hanging at their backs. Further to our left their long-bow men had shot almost as soon as ours, and I heard or seemed to hear the rush of the arrows through the apple-boughs and a man's cry therewith; but with us the long-bow had been before the crossbow; one of the arbalestiers fell outright, his great shield clattering down on him, and moved no more; while three others were hit and were crawling to the rear. The rest had

shouldered their bows and were aiming, but I thought
unsteadily; and before the triggers were drawn again
Will Green had nocked and loosed, and not a few
others of our folk; then came the wooden hail of the
bolts rattling through the boughs, but all overhead and
no one hit.

The next time Will Green nocked his arrow he drew
with a great shout, which all our fellows took up; for
the arbalestiers instead of turning about in their places
covered by their great shields and winding up their
crossbows for a second shot, as is the custom of such
soldiers, ran huddling together toward their men-at-
arms, our arrows driving thump-thump into their
shields as they ran: I saw four lying on the field dead
or sore wounded.

But our archers shouted again, and kept on each
plucking the arrows from the ground, and nocking and
loosing swiftly but deliberately at the line before them;
indeed now was the time for these terrible bowmen,
for as Will Green told me afterwards they always reck-
oned to kill through cloth or leather at five hundred
yards, and they had let the crossbow men come nearly
within three hundred, and these were now all mingled
and muddled up with the men-at-arms at scant five
hundred yards' distance; and belike, too, the latter were
not treating them too well, but seemed to be belaboring
them with their spear-staves in their anger at the poor-
ness of the play; so that as Will Green said it was like
shooting at hayricks.

All this you must understand lasted but a few minutes, and when our men had been shooting quite
coolly, like good workmen at peaceful work, for a few
minutes more, the enemy's line seemed to clear somewhat; the pennon with the three red kine showed in
front and three men armed from head to foot in
gleaming steel, except for their short coats bright with

heraldry, were with it. One of them (and he bore the three kine on his coat) turned round and gave some word of command, and an angry shout went up from them, and they came on steadily towards us, the man with the red kine on his coat leading them, a great naked sword in his hand: you must note that they were all on foot; but as they drew nearer I saw their horses led by grooms and pages coming on slowly behind them.

Sooth said Will Green that the men-at-arms run not fast either to or fro the fray; they came on no faster than a hasty walk, their arms clashing about them and the twang of the bows and whistle of the arrows never failing all the while, but going on like the push of the westerly gale, as from time to time the men-at-arms shouted, "Ha! ha! out! out! Kentish thieves!"

But when they began to fall on, Jack Straw shouted out, "Bills to the field! bills to the field!"

Then all our billmen ran up and leapt over the hedge into the meadow and stood stoutly along the ditch under our bows, Jack Straw in the forefront handling his great axe. Then he cast it into his left hand, caught up his horn and winded it loudly. The men-at-arms drew near steadily, some fell under the arrow-storm, but not a many; for though the target was big, it was hard, since not even the cloth-yard shaft could pierce well-wrought armor of plate, and there was much armor among them. Withal the arbalestiers were shooting again, but high and at a venture, so they did us no hurt.

But as these soldiers made wise by the French war were now drawing near, and our bowmen were casting down their bows and drawing their short swords, or handling their axes, as did Will Green, muttering, "Now must Hob Wright's gear end this play" — while this was a-doing, lo, on a sudden a flight of arrows from our right on the flank of the sergeants' array, which stayed them somewhat; not because it slew many men, but because they began to bethink them that their foes were many and all around them; then the road-hedge on the right seemed alive with armed men, for whatever could hold sword or staff amongst us was there; every bowman also leapt our orchard-hedge sword or axe in hand, and with a great shout, billmen, archers, and all, ran in on them; half-armed, yea, and half-naked some of them; strong and stout and lithe and light withal, the wrath of battle and the hope of better times lifting up their hearts till nothing could withstand them. So was all mingled together, and for a minute or two was a confused clamor over which rose a clatter like the riveting of iron plates, or the noise of the street of coppersmiths at Florence; then the throng burst open and the steel-clad sergeants and squires and knights ran huddling and shuffling to-wards their horses; but some cast down their weapons and threw up their hands and cried for peace and ransom; and some stood and fought desperately, and slew some till they were hammered down by many strokes, and of these were the bailiffs and tipstaves, and the lawyers and their men, who could not run and hoped for no mercy.

I looked as on a picture and wondered, and my mind was at strain to remember something forgotten, which yet had left its mark on it. I heard the noise of the horse-hoofs of the fleeing men-at-arms (the archers and arbalestiers had scattered before the last minutes of the play), I heard the confused sound of laughter and rejoicing down in the meadow, and close by me the evening wind lifting the lighter twigs of the trees, and far away the many noises of the quiet country, till light and sound both began to fade from me and I saw and heard nothing.

I leapt up to my feet presently and there was Will Green before me as I had first seen him in the street with coat and hood and the gear at his girdle and his unstrung bow in his hand; his face smiling and kind again, but maybe a thought sad.

"Well," quoth I, "what is the tale for the ballad-maker?"

"As Jack Straw said it would be," said he, "'the end of the day and the end of the fray;'" and he pointed to the brave show of the sky over the sunken sun; "the knights fled and the sheriff dead: two of the lawyer kind slain afield, and one hanged: and cruel was he to make them cruel: and three bailiffs knocked on the head — stout men, and so witless, that none found their brains in their skulls; and five arbalestiers and one archer slain, and a score and a half of others, mostly men come back from the French wars, men of the Companions there, knowing no other craft than fighting for gold; and this is the end they are paid for. Well, brother, saving the lawyers who belike had no souls, but only parchment deeds and libels of the same, God rest their souls!"

He fell a-musing; but I said, "And of our Fellowship were any slain?"

"Two good men of the township," he said, "Hob Horner and Antony Webber, were slain outright, Hob with a shaft and Antony in the hand-play, and John Pargetter hurt very sore on the shoulder with a glaive; and five more men of the Fellowship slain in the hand-play, and some few hurt, but not sorely. And as to those slain, if God give their souls rest it is well; for little rest they had on the earth belike; but for me, I desire rest no more."

I looked at him and our eyes met with no little love; and I wondered to see how wrath and grief within him were contending with the kindness of the man, and how clear the tokens of it were in his face.

"Come now, old lad," said he, "for I deem that John Ball and Jack Straw have a word to say to us at the cross yet, since these men broke off the telling of the tale; there shall we know what we are to take in hand tomorrow. And afterwards thou shalt eat and drink in my house this once, if never again."

So we went through the orchard closes again; and others were about and anigh us, all turned towards the cross as we went over the dewy grass, whereon the moon was just beginning to throw shadows.

Chapter VII

MORE WORDS AT THE CROSS

I got into my old place again on the steps of the cross, Will Green beside me, and above me John Ball and Jack Straw again. The moon was halfway up the heavens now, and the short summer night had begun, calm and fragrant, with just so much noise outside our quiet circle as made one feel the world alive and happy.

We waited silently until we had heard John Ball and the story of what was to do; and presently he began to speak.

"Good people, it is begun, but not ended. Which of you is hardy enough to wend the road to London tomorrow?"

"All! All!" they shouted.

"Yea," said he, "even so I deemed of you. Yet forsooth hearken! London is a great and grievous city; and mayhappen when ye come thither it shall seem to you overgreat to deal with, when ye remember the little townships and the cots ye came from.

"Moreover, when ye dwell here in Kent ye think

forsooth of your brethren in Essex or Suffolk, and there belike an end. But from London ye may have an inkling of all the world, and overburdensome maybe shall that seem to you, a few and a feeble people.

"Nevertheless I say to you, remember the Fellowship, in the hope of which ye have this day conquered; and when ye come to London be wise and wary; and that is as much as to say, be bold and hardy; for in these days are ye building a house which shall not be over-thrown, and the world shall not be too great or too little to hold it: for indeed it shall be the world itself, set free from evil-doers for friends to dwell in."

He ceased awhile, but they hearkened still, as if something more was coming. Then he said:

"Tomorrow we shall take the road for Rochester; and most like it were well to see what Sir John Newton in the castle may say to us: for the man is no ill man, and hath a tongue well-shaped for words; and it were well that we had him out of the castle and away with us, and that we put a word in his mouth to say to the King. And wot ye well, good fellows, that by then we come to Rochester we shall be a goodly company, and ere we come to Blackheath a very great company; and at London Bridge who shall stay our host?

"Therefore there is naught that can undo us except our own selves and our hearkening to soft words from those who would slay us. They shall bid us go home and abide peacefully with our wives and children while they, the lords and councilors and lawyers, imagine counsel and remedy for us; and even so shall our own folly bid us; and if we hearken thereto we are undone indeed; for they shall fall upon our peace with war, and our wives and children they shall take from us, and some of us they shall hang, and some they shall scourge, and the others shall be their yoke-beasts — yea, and worse, for they shall lack meat more.

"To fools hearken not, whether they be yourselves or your foemen, for either shall lead you astray.

"With the lords parley not, for ye know already what they would say to you, and that is, 'Churl, let me bridle thee and saddle thee, and eat thy livelihood that thou winnest, and call thee hard names because I eat thee up; and for thee, speak not and do not, save as I bid thee.'

"All that is the end of their parleying.

"Therefore be ye bold, and again bold, and thrice bold! Grip the bow, handle the staff, draw the sword, and set on in the name of the Fellowship!"

He ended amid loud shouts; but straightway answering shouts were heard, and a great noise of the winding of horns, and I misdoubted a new onslaught; and some of those in the throng began to string their bows and handle their bills; but Will Green pulled me by the sleeve and said:

"Friends are these by the winding of their horns; thou art quit for this night, old lad." And then Jack Straw cried out from the cross: "Fair and softly, my masters! These be men of our Fellowship, and are for your guests this night; they are from the bents this side of Medway, and are with us here because of the pilgrimage road, and that is the best in these parts, and so the shortest to Rochester. And doubt ye nothing of our being taken unawares this night; for I have bidden and sent out watchers of the ways, and neither a man's son nor a mare's son may come in on us without espial. Now make we our friends welcome. Forsooth, I looked for them an hour later; and had they come an hour earlier yet, some heads would now lie on the cold grass which shall lie on a feather bed tonight. But let be, since all is well!

"Now get we home to our houses, and eat and drink and slumber this night, if never once again, amid the multitude of friends and fellows; and yet soberly and without riot, since so much work is to hand. Moreover the priest saith, bear ye the dead men, both friends and foes, into the chancel of the church, and there this night he will wake them: but after tomorrow let the dead abide to bury their dead!"

Therewith he leapt down from the cross, and Will and I bestirred ourselves and mingled with the newcomers. They were some three hundred strong, clad and armed in all ways like the people of our township, except some half-dozen whose armor shone cold like ice under the moonbeams. Will Green soon had a dozen of them by the sleeve to come home with him to board and bed, and then I lost him for some minutes, and turning about saw John Ball standing behind me, looking pensively on all the stir and merry humors of the joyous uplanders.

"Brother from Essex," said he, "shall I see thee again tonight? I were fain of speech with thee; for thou seemest like one that has seen more than most."

"Yea," said I, "if ye come to Will Green's house, for thither am I bidden."

"Thither shall I come," said he, smiling kindly, "or no man I know in field. Lo you, Will Green looking for something, and that is me. But in his house will be song and the talk of many friends; and forsooth I have words in me that crave to come out in a quiet place where they may have each one his own answer. If thou art not afraid of dead men who were alive and wicked this morning, come thou to the church when supper is done, and there we may talk all we will."

Will Green was standing beside us before he had done, with his hand laid on the priest's shoulder, waiting till he had spoken out; and as I nodded Yea to John Ball he said:

"Now, master priest, thou hast spoken enough this

two or three hours, and this my new brother must tell and talk in my house; and there my maid will hear his wisdom which lay still under the hedge e'en now when the bolts were abroad. So come ye, and ye good fellows, come!"

So we turned away together into the little street. But while John Ball had been speaking to me I felt strangely, as though I had more things to say than the words I knew could make clear: as if I wanted to get from other people a new set of words. Moreover, as we passed up the street again I was once again smitten with the great beauty of the scene; the houses, the church with its new chancel and tower, snow-white in the moonbeams now; the dresses and arms of the people, men and women (for the latter were now mixed up with the men); their grave sonorous language, and the quaint and measured forms of speech, were again become a wonder to me and affected me almost to tears.

Chapter VIII

SUPPER AT WILL GREEN'S

I walked along with the others musing as if I did not belong to them, till we came to Will Green's house. He was one of the wealthier of the yeomen, and his house was one of those I told you of, the lower story of which was built of stone. It had not been built long, and was very trim and neat. The fit of wonder had worn off me again by then I reached it, or perhaps I should give you a closer description of it, for it was a handsome yeoman's dwelling of that day, which is as much as saying it was very beautiful. The house on the other side of it, the last house in the village, was old or even ancient; all built of stone, and except for a newer piece built on to it — a hall, it seemed — had round arches, some of them handsomely carved. I knew that this was the parson's house; but he was another sort of priest than John Ball, and what for fear, what for hatred, had gone back to his monastery with the two other chantrey priests who dwelt in that house; so that the men of the township, and more especially the women, were thinking gladly how John Ball should say mass in their new chancel on the morrow.

Will Green's daughter was waiting for him at the door and gave him a close and eager hug, and had a kiss to spare for each of us withal: a strong girl she was, as I have said, and sweet and wholesome also. She made merry with her father; yet it was easy to see that her heart was in her mouth all along. There was a younger girl some twelve summers old, and a lad of ten, who were easily to be known for his children; an old woman also, who had her livelihood there, and helped the household; and moreover three long young men, who came into the house after we had sat down, to whom Will nodded kindly. They were brisk lads and smart, but had been afield after the beasts that evening, and had not seen the fray.

The room we came into was indeed the house, for there was nothing but it on the ground floor, but a stair in the corner went up to the chamber or loft above. It was much like the room at the Rose, but bigger; the cupboard better wrought, and with more vessels on it, and handsomer. Also the walls, instead of being paneled, were hung with a coarse loosely-woven stuff of green worsted with birds and trees woven into it. There were flowers in plenty stuck about the room, mostly of the yellow blossoming flag or flower-de-luce, of which I had seen plenty in all the ditches, but in the window near the door was a pot full of those same white poppies I had seen when I first woke up; and the table was all set forth with meat and drink, a big salt-cellar of pewter in the middle, covered with a white cloth.

We sat down, the priest blessed the meat in the name of the Trinity, and we crossed ourselves and fell to. The victual was plentiful of broth and flesh-meat, and bread and cherries, so we ate and drank, and talked lightly together when we were full.

Yet was not the feast so gay as might have been. Will Green had me to sit next to him, and on the other side sat John Ball; but the priest had grown somewhat distraught, and sat as one thinking of somewhat that was like to escape his thought. Will Green looked at his daughter from time to time, and whiles his eyes glanced round the fair chamber as one who loved it, and his kind face grew sad, yet never sullen. When the herdsmen came into the hall they fell straightway to asking questions concerning those of the Fellowship who had been slain in the fray, and of their wives and children; so that for a while thereafter no man cared to jest, for they were a neighborly and kind folk, and were sorry both for the dead, and also for the living that should suffer from that day's work.

So then we sat silent awhile. The unseen moon was bright over the roof of the house, so that outside all was gleaming bright save the black shadows, though the moon came not into the room, and the white wall of the tower was the whitest and the brightest thing we could see.

Wide open were the windows, and the scents of the fragrant night floated in upon us, and the sounds of the men at their meat or making merry about the township; and whiles we heard the gibber of an owl from the trees westward of the church, and the sharp cry of a blackbird made fearful by the prowling stoat, or the far-off lowing of a cow from the upland pastures; or the hoofs of a horse trotting on the pilgrimage road (and one of our watchers would that be).

Thus we sat awhile, and once again came that feeling over me of wonder and pleasure at the strange and beautiful sights, mingled. with the sights and sounds and scents beautiful indeed, yet not strange, but rather long familiar to me.

But now Will Green started in his seat where he sat with his daughter hanging over his chair, her hand amidst his thick black curls, and she weeping softly, I thought; and his rough strong voice broke the silence.

"Why, lads and neighbors, what ails us? If the knights who fled from us this eve were to creep back hither and look in at the window, they would deem that they had slain us after all, and that we were but the ghosts of the men who fought them. Yet, forsooth, fair it is at whiles to sit with friends and let the summer night speak for us and tell us its tales. But now, sweetling, fetch the mazer and the wine."

"Forsooth," said John Ball, "if ye laugh not over-much now, ye shall laugh the more on the morrow of tomorrow, as ye draw nearer to the play of point and edge."

"That is sooth," said one of the upland guests. "So it was seen in France when we fought there; and the eve of fight was sober and the morn was merry."

"Yea," said another, "but there, forsooth, it was for nothing ye fought; and tomorrow it shall be for a fair reward."

"It was for life we fought," said the first.

"Yea," said the second, "for life; and leave to go home and find the lawyers at their fell game. Ho, Will Green, call a health over the cup!"

For now Will Green had a bowl of wine in his hand. He stood up and said: "Here, now, I call a health to the wrights of Kent who be turning our plow-shares into swords and our pruning-hooks into spears! Drink around, my masters!"

Then he drank, and his daughter filled the bowl brimming again and he passed it to me. As I took it I saw that it was of light polished wood curiously speckled, with a band of silver round it, on which was cut the legend, *"In the name of the Trinity fill the cup and drink to me.*" And before I drank, it came upon me to say, "Tomorrow, and the fair days afterwards!"

Then I drank a great draft of the strong red wine, and passed it on; and every man said something over it, as "The road to London Bridge!" "Hob Carter and his mate!" and so on, till last of all John Ball drank, saying:

"Ten years hence, and the freedom of the Fellowship!" Then he said to Will Green: "Now, Will, must I needs depart to go and wake the dead, both friend and foe in the church yonder; and whoso of you will be shriven let him come to me thither in the morn, nor spare for as little after sunrise as it may be. And this our friend and brother from over the water of Thames, he hath will to talk with me and I with him; so now will I take him by the hand: and so God keep you, fellows!"

I rose to meet him as he came round the head of the table, and took his hand. Will Green turned round to me and said:

"Thou wilt come back again timely, old lad; for betimes on the morrow must we rise if we shall dine at Rochester."

I stammered as I yea-said him; for John Ball was looking strangely at me with a half-smile, and my heart beat anxiously and fearfully: but we went quietly to the door and so out into the bright moonlight.

I lingered a little when we had passed the threshold, and looked back at the yellow-lighted window and the shapes of the men that I saw therein with a grief and longing that I could not give myself a reason for, since I was to come back so soon. John Ball did not press me to move forward, but held up his hand as if to bid me hearken. The folk and guests there had already shaken themselves down since our departure, and were gotten to be reasonably merry it seemed; for one of the

guests, he who had spoken of France before, had fallen
to singing a ballad of the war to a wild and melancholy
tune. I remember the first rhymes of it, which I heard
as I turned away my head and we moved on toward
the church:

"On a fair field of France
    We fought on a morning
    So lovely as it lieth
    Along by the water.
    There was many a lord there
    Mowed men in the medley,
    'Midst the banners of the barons
    And bold men of the knighthood,
    And spearmen and sergeants
    And shooters of the shaft."

Chapter IX

BETWIXT THE LIVING AND THE DEAD

*W*e entered the church through the south porch under a round-arched door carved very richly, and with a sculpture over the doorway and under the arch, which, as far as I could see by the moonlight, figured St. Michael and the Dragon. As I came into the rich gloom of the nave I noticed for the first time that I had one of those white poppies in my hand; I must have taken it out of the pot by the window as I passed out of Will Green's house.

The nave was not very large, but it looked spacious too; it was somewhat old, but well-built and handsome; the roof of curved wooden rafters with great tie-beams going from wall to wall. There was no light in it but that of the moon streaming through the windows, which were by no means large, and were glazed with white fretwork, with here and there a little figure in very deep rich colors. Two larger windows near the east end of each aisle had just been made so that the church

grew lighter toward the east, and I could see all the
work on the great screen between the nave and chancel
which glittered bright in new paint and gilding: a
candle glimmered in the loft above it, before the huge
rood that filled up the whole space between the loft
and the chancel arch. There was an altar at the east end
of each aisle, the one on the south side standing against
the outside wall, the one on the north against a traceried gaily-painted screen, for that aisle ran on along the
chancel. There were a few oak benches near this second
altar, seemingly just made, and well carved and
molded; otherwise the floor of the nave, which was
paved with a quaint pavement of glazed tiles like the
crocks I had seen outside as to ware, was quite clear,
and the shafts of the arches rose out of it white and
beautiful under the moon as though out of a sea, dark
but with gleams struck over it.

The priest let me linger and look round, when he
had crossed himself and given me the holy water; and
then I saw that the walls were figured all over with
stories, a huge St. Christopher with his black beard
looking like Will Green, being close to the porch by
which we entered, and above the chancel arch the
Doom of the last Day, in which the painter had not
spared either kings or bishops, and in which a lawyer
with his blue coif was one of the chief figures in the
group which the Devil was hauling off to hell.

"Yea," said John Ball, "'tis a goodly church and fair
as you may see 'twixt Canterbury and London as for
its kind; and yet do I misdoubt me where those who
are dead are housed, and where those shall house them
after they are dead, who built this house for God to
dwell in. God grant they be cleansed at last; forsooth
one of them who is now alive is a foul swine and a
cruel wolf. Art thou all so sure, scholar, that all such
have souls? and if it be so, was it well done of God to

make them? I speak to thee thus, for I think thou art no delator; and if thou be, why should I heed it, since I think not to come back from this journey."

I looked at him and, as it were, had some ado to answer him; but I said at last, "Friend, I never saw a soul, save in the body; I cannot tell."

He crossed himself and said, "Yet do I intend that ere many days are gone by my soul shall be in bliss among the fellowship of the saints, and merry shall it be, even before my body rises from the dead; for wisely I have wrought in the world, and I wot well of friends that are long ago gone from the world, as St. Martin, and St. Francis, and St. Thomas of Canterbury, who shall speak well of me to the heavenly Fellowship, and I shall in no wise lose my reward."

I looked shyly at him as he spoke; his face looked sweet and calm and happy, and I would have said no word to grieve him; and yet belike my eyes looked wonder on him: he seemed to note it and his face grew puzzled. "How deemest thou of these things?" said he: "why do men die else, if it be otherwise than this?"

I smiled: "Why then do they live?" said I.

Even in the white moonlight I saw his face flush, and he cried out in a great voice, "To do great deeds or to repent them that they ever were born."

"Yea," said I, "they live to live because the world liveth." He stretched out his hand to me and grasped mine, but said no more; and went on till we came to the door in the rood-screen; then he turned to me with his hand on the ring-latch, and said, "Hast thou seen many dead men?"

"Nay, but few," said I.

"And I a many," said he; "but come now and look on these, our friends first and then our foes, so that ye may not look to see them while we sit and talk of the days that are to be on the earth before the Day of Doom cometh."

So he opened the door, and we went into the chancel; a light burned on the high altar before the host, and looked red and strange in the moonlight that came through the wide traceried windows unstained by the pictures and beflowerings of the glazing; there were new stalls for the priests and vicars where we entered, carved more abundantly and beautifully than any of the woodwork I had yet seen, and everywhere was rich and fair color and delicate and dainty form. Our dead lay just before the high altar on low biers, their faces all covered with linen cloths, for some of them had been sore smitten and hacked in the fray. We went up to them and John Ball took the cloth from the face of one; he had been shot to the heart with a shaft and his face was calm and smooth. He had been a young man fair and comely, with hair flaxen almost to whiteness; he lay there in his clothes as he had fallen, the hands crossed over his breast and holding a rush cross. His bow lay on one side of him, his quiver of shafts and his sword on the other.

John Ball spake to me while he held the corner of the sheet: "What sayest thou, scholar? feelest thou sorrow of heart when thou lookest on this, either for the man himself, or for thyself and the time when thou shalt be as he is?"

I said, "Nay, I feel no sorrow for this; for the man is not here: this is an empty house, and the master has gone from it. Forsooth, this to me is but as a waxen image of a man; nay, not even that, for if it were an image, it would be an image of the man as he was when he was alive. But here is no life nor semblance of life, and I am not moved by it; nay, I am more moved by the man's clothes and war-gear — there is more life in them than in him."

"Thou sayest sooth," said he; "but sorrowest thou

not for thine own death when thou lookest on him?"

I said, "And how can I sorrow for that which I cannot so much as think of? Bethink thee that while I am alive I cannot think that I shall die, or believe in death at all, although I know well that I shall die — I can but think of myself as living in some new way."

Again he looked on me as if puzzled; then his face cleared as he said, "Yea, forsooth, and that is what the Church meaneth by death, and even that I look for; and that hereafter I shall see all the deeds that I have done in the body, and what they really were, and what shall come of them; and ever shall I be a member of the Church, and that is the Fellowship; then, even as now."

I sighed as he spoke; then I said, "Yea, somewhat in this fashion have most of men thought, since no man that is can conceive of not being; and I mind me that in those stories of the old Danes, their common word for a man dying is to say, 'He changed his life.'"

"And so deemest thou?"

I shook my head and said nothing.

"What hast thou to say hereon?" said he, "for there seemeth something betwixt us twain as it were a wall that parteth us."

"This," said I, "that though I die and end, yet mankind yet liveth, therefore I end not, since I am a man; and even so thou deemest, good friend; or at the least even so thou doest, since now thou art ready to die in grief and torment rather than be unfaithful to the Fellowship, yea rather than fail to work thine utmost for it; whereas, as thou thyself saidst at the cross, with a few words spoken and a little huddling-up of the truth, with a few pennies paid, and a few masses sung, thou mightest have had a good place on this earth and in that heaven. And as thou doest, so now doth many a poor man unnamed and unknown, and shall do while the world lasteth: and they that do less than this, fail because of fear, and are ashamed of their cowardice, and make many tales to themselves to deceive themselves, lest they should grow too much ashamed to live. And trust me if this were not so, the world would not live, but would die, smothered by its own stink. Is the wall betwixt us gone, friend?"

He smiled as he looked at me, kindly, but sadly and shamefast, and shook his head.

Then in a while he said, "Now ye have seen the images of those who were our friends, come and see the images of those who were once our foes."

So he led the way through the side screen into the chancel aisle, and there on the pavement lay the bodies of the foemen, their weapons taken from them and they stripped of their armor, but not otherwise of their clothes, and their faces mostly, but not all, covered. At the east end of the aisle was another altar, covered with a rich cloth beautifully figured, and on the wall over it was a deal of tabernacle work, in the midmost niche of it an image painted and gilt of a gay knight on horseback, cutting his own cloak in two with his sword to give a cantle of it to a half-naked beggar.

"Knowest thou any of these men?" said I.

He said, "Some I should know, could I see their faces; but let them be."

"Were they evil men?" said I.

"Yea," he said, "some two or three. But I will not tell thee of them; let St. Martin, whose house this is, tell their story if he will. As for the rest they were hapless fools, or else men who must earn their bread somehow, and were driven to this bad way of earning it; God rest their souls! I will be no tale-bearer, not even to God."

So we stood musing a little while, I gazing not on the dead men, but on the strange pictures on the wall, which were richer and deeper colored than those in the nave; till at last John Ball turned to me and laid his hand on my shoulder. I started and said, "Yea, brother; now must I get me back to Will Green's house, as I promised to do so timely."

"Not yet, brother," said he; "I have still much to say to thee, and the night is yet young. Go we and sit in the stalls of the vicars, and let us ask and answer on matters concerning the fashion of this world of men-folk, and of this land wherein we dwell; for once more I deem of thee that thou hast seen things which I have not seen, and could not have seen." With that word he led me back into the chancel, and we sat down side by side in the stalls at the west end of it, facing the high altar and the great east window. By this time the chancel was getting dimmer as the moon wound round the heavens; but yet was there a twilight of the moon, so that I could still see the things about me for all the brightness of the window that faced us; and this moon twilight would last, I knew, until the short summer night should wane, and the twilight of the dawn begin to show us the colors of all things about us.

So we sat, and I gathered my thoughts to hear what he would say, and I myself was trying to think what I should ask of him; for I thought of him as he of me, that he had seen things which I could not have seen.

Chapter X

TWO TALK OF THE DAYS TO COME

"Brother," said John Ball, "how deemest thou of our adventure? I do not ask thee if thou thinkest we are right to play the play like men, but whether playing like men we shall fail like men."

"Why dost thou ask me?" said I; "how much further than beyond this church can I see?"

"Far further," quoth he, "for I wot that thou art a scholar and hast read books; and withal, in some way that I cannot name, thou knowest more than we; as though with thee the world had lived longer than with us. Hide not, therefore, what thou hast in thine heart, for I think after this night I shall see thee no more, until we meet in the heavenly Fellowship."

"Friend," I said, "ask me what thou wilt; or rather ask thou the years to come to tell thee some little of their tale; and yet methinks thou thyself mayest have some deeming thereof."

He raised himself on the elbow of the stall and looked me full in the face, and said to me: "Is it so after all that thou art no man in the flesh, but art sent to me by the Master of the Fellowship, and the King's Son of Heaven, to tell me what shall be? If that be so tell me straight out, since I had some deeming hereof before; whereas thy speech is like ours and yet unlike, and thy face hath something in it which is not after the fashion of our day. And yet take heed, if thou art such an one, I fear thee not, nay, nor him that sent thee; nor for thy bidding, nor for his, will I turn back from London Bridge but will press on, for I do what is meet and right."

"Nay," said I, "did I not tell thee e'en now that I knew life but not death? I am not dead; and as to who hath sent me, I say not that I am come by my own will; for I know not; yet also I know not the will that hath sent me hither. And this I say to thee, moreover, that if I know more than thou, I do far less; therefore thou art my captain and I thy minstrel."

He sighed as one from whom a weight had been lifted, and said: "Well, then, since thou art alive on the earth and a man like myself, tell me how deemest thou of our adventure: shall we come to London, and how shall we fare there?"

Said I, "What shall hinder you to come to London, and to fare there as ye will? For be sure that the Fellowship in Essex shall not fail you; nor shall the Londoners who hate the king's uncles withstand you; nor hath the Court any great force to meet you in the field; ye shall cast fear and trembling into their hearts."

"Even so, I thought," said he; "but afterwards what shall betide?"

Said I, "It grieves my heart to say that which I think. Yet hearken; many a man's son shall die who is now alive and happy, and if the soldiers be slain, and of them most not on the field, but by the lawyers, how shall the captains escape? Surely thou goest to thy death."

He smiled very sweetly, yet proudly, as he said: "Yea, the road is long, but the end cometh at last. Friend, many a day have I been dying; for my sister, with whom I have played and been merry in the autumn tide about the edges of the stubble — fields; and we gathered the nuts and bramble-berries there, and started thence the missel-thrush, and wondered at his voice and thought him big; and the sparrow-hawk wheeled and turned over the hedges and the weasel ran across the path, and the sound of the sheep-bells came to us from the downs as we sat happy on the grass; and she is dead and gone from the earth, for she pined from famine after the years of the great sickness; and my brother was slain in the French wars, and none thanked him for dying save he that stripped him of his gear; and my unwedded wife with whom I dwelt in love after I had taken the tonsure, and all men said she was good and fair, and true she was and lovely; she also is dead and gone from the earth; and why should I abide save for the deeds of the flesh which must be done? Truly, friend, this is but an old tale that men must die; and I will tell thee another, to wit, that they live: and I live now and shall live. Tell me then what shall befall."

Somehow I could not heed him as a living man as much as I had done, and the voice that came from me seemed less of me as I answered:

"These men are strong and valiant as any that have been or shall be, and good fellows also and kindly; but they are simple, and see no great way before their own noses. The victory shall they have and shall not know what to do with it; they shall fight and overcome, because of their lack of knowledge, and because of their lack of knowledge shall they be cozened and betrayed when their captains are slain, and all shall come to naught by seeming; and the king's uncles shall prevail, that both they and the king may come to the shame that is appointed for them. And yet when the lords have vanquished, and all England lieth under them again, yet shall their victory be fruitless; for the free men that hold unfree lands shall they not bring under the collar again, and villeinage shall slip from their hands, till there be, and not long after ye are dead, but few unfree men in England; so that your lives and your deaths both shall bear fruit."

"Said I not," quoth John Ball, "that thou wert a sending from other times? Good is thy message, for the land shall be free. Tell on now."

He spoke eagerly, and I went on somewhat sadly: "The times shall better, though the king and lords shall worsen, the Gilds of Craft shall wax and become mightier; more recourse shall there be of foreign merchants. There shall be plenty in the land and not famine. Where a man now earneth two pennies he shall earn three."

"Yea," said he, "then shall those that labor become strong and stronger, and so soon shall it come about that all men shall work and none make to work, and so shall none be robbed, and at last shall all men labor and live and be happy, and have the goods of the earth without money and without price."

"Yea," said I, "that shall indeed come to pass, but not yet for a while, and belike a long while."

And I sat for long without speaking, and the church grew darker as the moon waned yet more.

Then I said: "Bethink thee that these men shall yet have masters over them, who have at hand many a law and custom for the behoof of masters, and being masters can make yet more laws in the same behoof; and they shall suffer poor people to thrive just so long as their thriving shall profit the mastership and no longer; and so shall it be in those days I tell of; for there shall be king and lords and knights and squires still, with servants to do their bidding, and make honest men afraid; and all these will make nothing and eat much as aforetime, and the more that is made in the land the more shall they crave."

"Yea," said he, "that wot I well, that these are of the kin of the daughters of the horse-leech; but how shall they slake their greed, seeing that as thou sayest villein-age shall be gone? Belike their men shall pay them quit-rents and do them service, as free men may, but all this according to law and not beyond it; so that though the workers shall be richer than they now be, the lords shall be no richer, and so all shall be on the road to being free and equal."

Said I, "Look you, friend; aforetime the lords, for the most part, held the land and all that was on it, and the men that were on it worked for them as their horses worked, and after they were fed and housed all was the lords'; but in the time to come the lords shall see their men thriving on the land and shall say once more, 'These men have more than they need, why have we not the surplus since we are their lords?' Moreover, in those days shall betide much chaffering for wares be-tween man and man, and country and country; and the lords shall note that if there were less corn and less men on their lands there would be more sheep, that is to say more wool for chaffer, and that thereof they should have abundantly more than aforetime; since all the land they own, and it pays them quit-rent or service, save here and there a croft or a close of a yeoman; and all this might grow wool for them to sell to the Easter-lings. Then shall England see a new thing, for whereas hitherto men have lived on the land and by it, the land shall no longer need them, but many sheep and a few shepherds shall make wool grow to be sold for money to the Easterlings, and that money shall the lords pouch: for, look you, they shall set the lawyers a-work and the strong hand moreover, and the land they shall take to themselves and their sheep; and except for these lords of land few shall be the free men that shall hold a rood of land whom the word of their lord may not turn adrift straightway."

"How mean you?" said John Ball: "shall all men be villeins again?"

"Nay," said I, "there shall be no villeins in England."

"Surely then," said he, "it shall be worse, and all men save a few shall be thralls to be bought and sold at the cross."

"Good friend," said I, "it shall not be so; all men shall be free even as ye would have it; yet, as I say, few indeed shall have so much land as they can stand upon save by buying such a grace of their masters."

"And now," said he, "I wot not what thou sayest. I know a thrall, and he is his master's every hour, and never his own; and a villein I know, and whiles he is his own and whiles his lord's; and I know a free man, and he is his own always; but how shall he be his own if he have naught whereby to make his livelihood? Or shall he be a thief and take from others? Then is he an outlaw. Wonderful is this thou tellest of a free man with naught whereby to live!"

"Yet so it shall be," said I, "and by such free men shall all wares be made."

"Nay, that cannot be; thou art talking riddles," said he; "for how shall a woodwright make a chest without the wood and the tools?"

Said I, "He must needs buy leave to labor of them that own all things except himself and such as himself."

"Yea, but wherewith shall he buy it?" said John Ball.

"What hath he except himself?"

"With himself then shall he buy it," quoth I, "with his body and the power of labor that lieth therein; with the price of his labor shall he buy leave to labor."

"Riddles again!" said he; "how can he sell his labor for aught else but his daily bread? He must win by his labor meat and drink and clothing and housing! Can he sell his labor twice over?"

"Not so," said I, "but this shall he do belike; he shall sell himself, that is the labor that is in him, to the master that suffers him to work, and that master shall give to him from out of the wares he maketh enough to keep him alive, and to beget children and nourish them till they be old enough to be sold like himself, and the residue shall the rich man keep to himself."

John Ball laughed aloud, and said: "Well, I perceive we are not yet out of the land of riddles. The man may well do what thou sayest and live, but he may not do it and live a free man."

"Thou sayest sooth," said I.

Chapter XI

HARD IT IS FOR THE OLD WORLD TO SEE THE NEW.

*H*e held his peace awhile, and then he said: "But no man selleth himself and his children into thralldom uncompelled; nor is any fool so great a fool as willingly to take the name of freeman and the life of a thrall as payment for the very life of a freeman. Now would I ask thee somewhat else; and I am the readier to do so since I perceive that thou art a wondrous seer; for surely no man could of his own wit have imagined a tale of such follies as thou hast told me. Now well I wot that men having once shaken themselves clear of the burden of villeinage, as thou sayest we shall do (and I bless thee for the word), shall never bow down to this worser tyranny without sore strife in the world; and surely so sore shall it be, before our valiant sons give way, that maids and little lads shall take the sword and the spear, and in many a field men's blood and not water shall turn the gristmills of England. But when all this is over, and the tyranny is established, because there are but few men in the land after the great war, how shall it be with you then? Will there not be many soldiers and sergeants and few workers? Surely in every parish ye shall have the constables to see that the men work; and they shall be saying every day, 'Such an one, hast thou yet sold thyself for this day or this week or this year? Go to now, and get thy bargain done, or it shall be the worse for thee.' And wheresoever work is going on there shall be constables again, and those that labor shall labor under the whip like the Hebrews in the land of Egypt. And every man that may, will steal as a dog snatches at a bone; and there again shall ye need more soldiers and more constables till the land is eaten up by them; nor shall the lords and the masters even be able to bear the burden of it; nor will their gains be so great, since that which each man may do in a day is not right great when all is said."

"Friend," said I, "from thine own valiancy and high heart thou speakest, when thou sayest that they who fall under this tyranny shall fight to the death against it. Wars indeed there shall be in the world, great and grievous, and yet few on this score; rather shall men fight as they have been fighting in France at the bidding of some lord of the manor, or some king, or at last at the bidding of some usurer and forestaller of the market. Valiant men, forsooth, shall arise in the beginning of these evil times, but though they shall die as ye shall, yet shall not their deaths be fruitful as yours shall be; because ye, forsooth, are fighting against villeinage which is waning, but they shall fight against usury which is waxing. And, moreover, I have been telling thee how it shall be when the measure of the time is full; and we, looking at these things from afar, can see them as they are indeed; but they who live at the beginning of those times and amidst them, shall not know what is doing around them; they shall indeed feel the plague and yet not know the remedy; by little and by little they shall fall from their better livelihood, and weak and helpless shall they grow, and have no might to withstand the evil of this tyranny; and then again when the times mend somewhat and they have but a little more ease, then shall it be to them like the kingdom of heaven, and they shall have no will to withstand any tyranny, but shall think themselves happy that they be pinched somewhat less. Also whereas thou sayest that there shall be forever constables and sergeants going to and fro to drive men to work, and that they will not work save under the lash, thou art wrong and it shall not be so; for there shall ever be more workers than the masters may set to work, so that men shall strive eagerly for leave to work; and when one says, I will sell my hours at such and such a price, then another will say, and I for so much less; so that never shall the lords lack slaves willing to work, but often the slaves shall lack lords to buy them."

"Thou tellest marvels indeed," said he; "but how then? if all the churls work not, shall there not be famine and lack of wares?"

"Famine enough," said I, "yet not from lack of wares; it shall be clean contrary. What wilt thou say when I tell thee that in the latter days there shall be such traffic and such speedy travel across the seas that most wares shall be good cheap, and bread of all things the cheapest?"

Quoth he: "I should say that then there would be better livelihood for men, for in times of plenty it is well; for then men eat that which their own hands have harvested, and need not to spend of their substance in buying of others. Truly, it is well for honest men, but not so well for forestallers and regraters; but who heeds what befalls such foul swine, who filch the money from people's purses, and do not one hair's turn of work to help them?" Forestaller, one who buys up goods when they are cheap, and so raises the price for his own benefit; forestalls the due and real demand. Regrater, one who both buys and sells in the same market, or within five miles thereof; buys, say a ton of cheese at 10 A.M. and sells it at 5 P.M. a penny a pound dearer without moving from his chair. The word "monopolist" will cover both species of thief.

"Yea, friend," I said, "but in those latter days all power shall be in the hands of these foul swine, and they shall be the rulers of all; therefore, hearken, for I tell thee that times of plenty shall in those days be the times of famine, and all shall pray for the prices of wares to rise, so that the forestallers and regraters may thrive, and that some of their well-doing may overflow on to those on whom they live."

"I am weary of thy riddles," he said. "Yet at least I hope that there may be fewer and fewer folk in the land; as may well be, if life is then so foul and wretched."

"Alas, poor man!" I said; "nor mayst thou imagine how foul and wretched it may be for many of the folk; and yet I tell thee that men shall increase and multiply, till where there is one man in the land now, there shall be twenty in those days — yea, in some places ten times twenty."

"I have but little heart to ask thee more questions," said he; "and when thou answerest, thy words are plain, but the things they tell of I may scarce understand. But tell me this: in those days will men deem that so it must be forever, as great men even now tell us of our ills, or will they think of some remedy?"

I looked about me. There was but a glimmer of light in the church now, but what there was, was no longer the strange light of the moon, but the first coming of the kindly day.

"Yea," said John Ball, "'tis the twilight of the dawn. God and St. Christopher send us a good day!"

"John Ball," said I, "I have told thee that thy death will bring about that which thy life has striven for: thinkest thou that the thing which thou strivest for is worth the labor? or dost thou believe in the tale I have told thee of the days to come?"

He said: "I tell thee once again that I trust thee for a seer; because no man could make up such a tale as thou; the things which thou tellest are too wonderful for a minstrel, the tale too grievous. And whereas thou askest as to whether I count my labor lost, I say nay; if so be that in those latter times (and worser than ours they will be) men shall yet seek a remedy: therefore again I ask thee, is it so that they shall?"

"Yea," said I, "and their remedy shall be the same as thine, although the days be different: for if the folk be enthralled, what remedy save that they be set free? and if they have tried many roads towards freedom, and found that they led no-whither, then shall they try yet another. Yet in the days to come they shall be slothful to try it, because their masters shall be so much mightier than thine, that they shall not need to show the high hand, and until the days get to their evilest, men shall be cozened into thinking that it is of their own free will that they must needs buy leave to labor by pawning their labor that is to be. Moreover, your lords and masters seem very mighty to you, each one of them, and so they are, but they are few; and the masters of the days to come shall not each one of them seem very mighty to the men of those days, but they shall be very many, and they shall be of one intent in these matters without knowing it; like as one sees the oars of a galley when the rowers are hidden, that rise and fall as it were with one will."

"And yet," he said, "shall it not be the same with

those that these men devour? shall not they also have one will?"

"Friend," I said, "they shall have the will to live, as the wretchedest thing living has: therefore shall they sell themselves that they may live, as I told thee; and their hard need shall be their lord's easy livelihood, and because of it he shall sleep without fear, since their need compelleth them not to loiter by the way to lament with friend or brother that they are pinched in their servitude, or to devise means for ending it. And yet indeed thou sayest it: they also shall have one will if they but knew it: but for a long while they shall have but a glimmer of knowledge of it: yet doubt it not that in the end they shall come to know it clearly, and then shall they bring about the remedy; and in those days shall it be seen that thou hast not wrought for nothing, because thou hast seen beforehand what the remedy should be, even as those of later days have seen it."

We both sat silent a little while. The twilight was gaining on the night, though slowly. I looked at the poppy which I still held in my hand, and bethought me of Will Green, and said:

"Lo, how the light is spreading: now must I get me back to Will Green's house as I promised."

"Go, then," said he, "if thou wilt. Yet meseems before long he shall come to us; and then mayst thou sleep among the trees on the green grass till the sun is high, for the host shall not be on foot very early; and sweet it is to sleep in shadow by the sun in the full morning when one has been awake and troubled through the night-tide."

"Yet I will go now," said I; "I bid thee good-night, or rather good-morrow."

Therewith I half rose up; but as I did so the will to depart left me as though I had never had it, and I sat down again, and heard the voice of John Ball, at first as one speaking from far away, but little by little growing nearer and more familiar to me, and as if once more it were coming from the man himself whom I had got to know.

Chapter XII

ILL WOULD CHANGE BE AT WHILES WERE IT NOT FOR THE CHANGE BEYOND THE CHANGE

*H*e said: "Many strange things hast thou told me that I could not understand; yea, some my wit so failed to compass, that I cannot so much as ask thee questions concerning them; but of some matters would I ask thee, and I must hasten, for in very sooth the night is worn old and grey. Whereas thou sayest that in the days to come, when there shall be no laboring men who are not thralls after their new fashion, that their lords shall be many and very many, it seemeth to me that these same lords, if they be many, shall hardly be rich, or but very few of them, since they must verily feed and clothe and house their thralls, so that that which they take from them, since it will have to be dealt out amongst many, will not be enough to make many rich;

since out of one man ye may get but one man's work; and pinch him never so sorely, still as aforesaid ye may not pinch him so sorely as not to feed him. Therefore, though the eyes of my mind may see a few lords and many slaves, yet can they not see many lords as well as many slaves; and if the slaves be many and the lords few, then some day shall the slaves make an end of that mastery by the force of their bodies. How then shall thy mastership of the latter days endure?"

"John Ball," said I, "mastership hath many shifts whereby it striveth to keep itself alive in the world. And now hear a marvel: whereas thou sayest these two times that out of one man ye may get but one man's work, in days to come one man shall do the work of a hundred men — yea, of a thousand or more: and this is the shift of mastership that shall make many masters and many rich men."

John Ball laughed. "Great is my harvest of riddles tonight," said he; "for even if a man sleep not, and eat and drink while he is a-working, ye shall but make two men, or three at the most, out of him."

Said I: "Sawest thou ever a weaver at his loom?"

"Yea," said he, "many a time."

He was silent a little, and then said: "Yet I marveled not at it; but now I marvel, because I know what thou wouldst say. Time was when the shuttle was thrust in and out of all the thousand threads of the warp, and it was long to do; but now the spring-staves go up and down as the man's feet move, and this and that leaf of the warp cometh forward and the shuttle goeth in one shot through all the thousand warps. Yea, so it is that this multiplieth a man many times. But look you, he is so multiplied already; and so hath he been, meseemeth, for many hundred years."

"Yea," said I, "but what hitherto needed the masters to multiply him more? For many hundred years the workman was a thrall bought and sold at the cross; and for other hundreds of years he hath been a villein — that is, a working-beast and a part of the stock of the manor on which he liveth; but then thou and the like of thee shall free him, and then is mastership put to its shifts; for what should avail the mastery then, when the master no longer owneth the man by law as his chattel, nor any longer by law owneth him as stock of his land, if the master hath not that which he on whom he liveth may not lack and live withal, and cannot have without selling himself?"

He said nothing, but I saw his brow knitted and his lips pressed together as though in anger; and again I said:

"Thou hast seen the weaver at his loom: think how it should be if he sit no longer before the web and cast the shuttle and draw home the sley, but if the shed open of itself and the shuttle of itself speed through it as swift as the eye can follow, and the sley come home of itself; and the weaver standing by and whistling *The Hunt's Up!* the while, or looking to half-a-dozen looms and bidding them what to do. And as with the weaver so with the potter, and the smith, and every worker in metals, and all other crafts, that it shall be for them looking on and tending, as with the man that sitteth in the cart while the horse draws. Yea, at last so shall it be even with those who are mere husbandmen; and no longer shall the reaper fare afield in the morning with his hook over his shoulder, and smite and bind and smite again till the sun is down and the moon is up; but he shall draw a thing made by men into the field with one or two horses, and shall say the word and the horses shall go up and down, and the thing shall reap and gather and bind, and do the work of many men. Imagine all this in thy mind if thou canst, at least as ye may imagine a tale of enchantment told by a minstrel, and then tell me what shouldst thou deem that the life of men would be amidst all this, men such as these men of the township here, or the men of the Canterbury gilds."

"Yea," said he; "but before I tell thee my thoughts of thy tale of wonder, I would ask thee this: In those days when men work so easily, surely they shall make more wares than they can use in one countryside, or one good town, whereas in another, where things have not gone as well, they shall have less than they need; and even so it is with us now, and thereof cometh scarcity and famine; and if people may not come at each other's goods, it availeth the whole land little that one countryside hath more than enough while another hath less; for the goods shall abide there in the storehouses of the rich place till they perish. So if that be so in the days of wonder ye tell of (and I see not how it can be otherwise), then shall men be but little holpen by making all their wares so easily and with so little labor."

I smiled again and said: "Yea, but it shall not be so; not only shall men be multiplied a hundred and a thousand fold, but the distance of one place from another shall be as nothing; so that the wares which lie ready for market in Durham in the evening may be in London on the morrow morning; and the men of Wales may eat corn of Essex and the men of Essex wear wool of Wales; so that, so far as the flitting of goods to market goes, all the land shall be as one parish. Nay, what say I? Not as to this land only shall it be so, but even the Indies, and far countries of which thou knowest not, shall be, so to say, at every man's door, and wares which now ye account precious and dear-bought, shall then be common things bought and sold for little price at every huckster's stall. Say then, John, shall not those days be merry, and plentiful of ease and contentment for all men?"

"Brother," said he, "meseemeth some doleful mockery lieth under these joyful tidings of thine; since thou hast already partly told me to my sad bewilderment what the life of man shall be in those days. Yet will I now for a little set all that aside to consider thy strange tale as of a minstrel from over sea, even as thou biddest me. Therefore I say, that if men still abide men as I have known them, and unless these folk of England change as, the land changeth — and forsooth of the men, for good and for evil, I can think no other than I think now, or behold them other than I have known them and loved them — I say if the men be still men, what will happen except that there should be all plenty in the land, and not one poor man therein, unless of his own free will he choose to lack and be poor, as a man in religion or such like; for there would then be such abundance of all good things, that, as greedy as the lords might be, there would be enough to satisfy their greed and yet leave good living for all who labored with their hands; so that these should labor far less than now, and they would have time to learn knowledge, so that there should be no learned or unlearned, for all should be learned; and they would have time also to learn how to order the matters of the parish and the hundred, and of the parliament of the realm, so that the king should take no more than his own; and to order the rule of the realm, so that all men, rich and unrich, should have part therein; and so by undoing of evil laws and making of good ones, that fashion would come to an end whereof thou speakest, that rich men make laws for their own behoof; for they should no longer be able to do thus when all had part in making the laws; whereby it would soon come about that there would be no men rich and tyrannous, but all should have enough and to spare of the increase of the earth and the work of their own hands. Yea surely, brother, if ever it cometh about that men shall be able to make things, and not men, work for their superfluities, and that the length of travel from one place to another be made of no account, and all the world be a market for all the world, then all shall live in health and wealth; and envy and grudging shall perish. For then shall we have conquered the earth and it shall be enough; and then shall the kingdom of heaven be come down to the earth in very deed. Why lookest thou so sad and sorry? what sayest thou?"

I said: "Hast thou forgotten already what I told thee, that in those latter days a man who hath naught save his own body (and such men shall be far the most of men) must needs pawn his labor for leave to labor? Can such a man be wealthy? Hast thou not called him a thrall?"

"Yea," he said; "but how could I deem that such things could be when those days should be come wherein men could make things work for them?"

"Poor man!" said I. "Learn that in those very days, when it shall be with the making of things as with the carter in the cart, that there he sitteth and shaketh the reins and the horse draweth and the cart goeth; in those days, I tell thee, many men shall be as poor and wretched always, year by year, as they are with thee when there is famine in the land; nor shall any have plenty and surety of livelihood save those that shall sit by and look on while others labor; and these, I tell thee, shall be a many, so that they shall see to the making of all laws, and in their hands shall be all power, and the laborers shall think that they cannot do without these men that live by robbing them, and shall praise them and well-nigh pray to them as ye pray to the saints, and the best worshipped man in the land shall be he who by forestalling and regrating hath gotten to him the most money."

"Yea," said he, "and shall they who see themselves robbed worship the robber? Then indeed shall men be changed from what they are now, and they shall be sluggards, dolts, and cowards beyond all the earth hath yet borne. Such are not the men I have known in my life-days, and that now I love in my death."

"Nay," I said, "but the robbery shall they not see; for have I not told thee that they shall hold themselves to be free men? And for why? I will tell thee: but first tell me how it fares with men now; may the laboring man become a lord?"

He said: "The thing hath been seen that churls have risen from the dortoir of the monastery to the abbot's chair and the bishop's throne; yet not often; and whiles hath a bold sergeant become a wise captain, and they have made him squire and knight; and yet but very seldom. And now I suppose thou wilt tell me that the Church will open her arms wider to this poor people, and that many through her shall rise into lordship. But what availeth that? Naught were it to me if the Abbot of St. Alban's with his golden miter sitting guarded by his knights and sergeants, or the Prior of Merton with his hawks and his hounds, had once been poor men, if they were now tyrants of poor men; nor would it better the matter if there were ten times as many Houses of Religion in the land as now are, and each with a churl's son for abbot or prior over it."

I smiled and said: "Comfort thyself; for in those days shall there be neither abbey nor priory in the land, nor monks nor friars, nor any religious." (He started as I spoke.) "But thou hast told me that hardly in these days may a poor man rise to be a lord: now I tell thee that in the days to come poor men shall be able to become lords and masters and do-nothings; and oft will it be seen that they shall do so; and it shall be even for that cause that their eyes shall be blinded to the robbing of themselves by others, because they shall hope in their souls that they may each live to rob others: and this shall be the very safeguard of all rule and law in those days."

"Now am I sorrier than thou hast yet made me," said he; "for when once this is established, how then can it be changed? Strong shall be the tyranny of the latter days. And now meseems, if thou sayest sooth, this time of the conquest of the earth shall not bring heaven down to the earth, as erst I deemed it would, but rather that it shall bring hell up on to the earth. Woe's me, brother, for thy sad and weary foretelling! And yet saidst thou that the men of those days would seek a remedy. Canst thou yet tell me, brother, what that remedy shall be, lest the sun rise upon me made hopeless by thy tale of what is to be? And, lo you, soon shall she rise upon the earth."

In truth the dawn was widening now, and the colors coming into the pictures on wall and in window; and as well as I could see through the varied glazing of these last (and one window before me had as yet nothing but white glass in it), the ruddy glow, which had but so little a while quite died out in the west, was now beginning to gather in the east — the new day was beginning. I looked at the poppy that I still carried in my hand, and it seemed to me to have withered and dwindled. I felt anxious to speak to my companion and tell him much, and withal I felt that I must hasten, or for some reason or other I should be too late; so I spoke at last loud and hurriedly:

"John Ball, be of good cheer; for once more thou knowest, as I know, that the Fellowship of Men shall endure, however many tribulations it may have to wear through. Look you, a while ago was the light bright about us; but it was because of the moon, and the night was deep notwithstanding, and when the moonlight waned and died, and there was but a little glimmer in place of the bright light, yet was the world glad because all things knew that the glimmer was of day and not of night. Lo you, an image of the times to betide the hope of the Fellowship of Men. Yet forsooth, it may well be that this bright day of summer which is now dawning upon us is no image of the beginning of the day that shall be; but rather shall that day-dawn be cold and grey and surly; and yet by its light shall men see things as they verily are, and no longer enchanted by the gleam of the moon and the glamour of the dream-tide. By such grey light shall wise men and valiant souls see the remedy, and deal with it, a real thing that may be touched and handled, and no glory of the heavens to be worshipped from afar off. And what shall it be, as I told thee before, save that men shall be determined to be free; yea, free as thou wouldst have them, when thine hope rises the highest, and thou art thinking not of the king's uncles, and poll-groat bailiffs, and the villeinage of Essex, but of the end of all, when men shall have the fruits of the earth and the fruits of their toil thereon, without money and without price. The time shall come, John Ball, when that dream of thine that this shall one day be, shall be a thing that men shall talk of soberly, and as a thing soon to come about, as even with thee they talk of the villeins becoming tenants paying their lord quit-rent; therefore, hast thou done well to hope it; and, if thou heedest this also, as I suppose thou heedest it little, thy name shall abide by thy hope in those days to come, and thou shalt not be forgotten."

I heard his voice come out of the twilight, scarcely seeing him, though now the light was growing fast, as he said:

"Brother, thou givest me heart again; yet since now I wot well that thou art a sending from far-off times and far-off things: tell thou, if thou mayest, to a man who is going to his death how this shall come about."

"Only this may I tell thee," said I; "to thee, when thou didst try to conceive of them, the ways of the days to come seemed follies scarce to be thought of; yet shall they come to be familiar things, and an order by which every man liveth, ill as he liveth, so that men shall deem of them, that thus it hath been since the beginning of the world, and that thus it shall be while the world endureth; and in this wise so shall they be thought of a long while; and the complaint of the poor the rich man shall heed, even as much and no more as he who lieth in pleasure under the lime trees in the summer heedeth the murmur of his toiling bees. Yet in time shall this also grow old, and doubt shall creep in, because men shall scarce be able to live by that order, and the complaint of the poor shall be hearkened, no longer as a tale not utterly grievous, but as a threat of ruin, and a fear. Then shall these things, which to thee seem follies, and to the men between thee and me mere wisdom and the bond of stability, seem follies once again; yet, whereas men have so long lived by them, they shall cling to them yet from blindness and from fear; and those that see, and that have thus much conquered fear that they are furthering the real time that cometh and not the dream that faileth, these men shall the blind and the fearful mock and missay, and torment and murder: and great and grievous shall be the strife in those days, and many the failures of the wise, and too oft sore shall be the despair of the valiant; and back-sliding, and doubt, and contest between friends and fellows lacking time in the hubbub to understand each other, shall grieve many hearts and hinder the Host of the Fellowship: yet shall all bring about the end, till thy deeming of folly and ours shall be one, and thy hope and our hope; and then — the

Day will have come."

Once more I heard the voice of John Ball: "Now, brother, I say farewell; for now verily hath the Day of the Earth come, and thou and I are lonely of each other again; thou hast been a dream to me as I to thee, and sorry and glad have we made each other, as tales of old time and the longing of times to come shall ever make men to be. I go to life and to death, and leave thee; and scarce do I know whether to wish thee some dream of the days beyond thine to tell what shall be, as thou hast told me, for I know not if that shall help or hinder thee; but since we have been kind and very friends, I will not leave thee without a wish of good-will, so at least I wish thee what thou thyself wishest for thyself, and that is hopeful strife and blameless peace, which is to say in one word, life. Farewell, friend."

For some little time, although I had known that the daylight was growing and what was around me, I had scarce seen the things I had before noted so keenly; but now in a flash I saw all — the east crimson with sunrise through the white window on my right hand; the richly-carved stalls and gilded screen work, the pictures on the walls, the loveliness of the faultless color of the mosaic window lights, the altar and the red light over it looking strange in the daylight, and the biers with the hidden dead men upon them that lay before the high altar. A great pain filled my heart at the sight of all that beauty, and withal I heard quick steps coming up the paved church-path to the porch, and the loud whistle of a sweet old tune therewith; then the footsteps stopped at the door; I heard the latch rattle, and knew that Will Green's hand was on the ring of it.

Then I strove to rise up, but fell back again; a white light, empty of all sights, broke upon me for a moment, and lo I behold, I was lying in my familiar bed, the southwesterly gale rattling the Venetian blinds and making their hold-fasts squeak.

I got up presently, and going to the window looked out on the winter morning; the river was before me broad between outer bank and bank, but it was nearly dead ebb, and there was a wide space of mud on each side of the hurrying stream, driven on the faster as it seemed by the push of the southwest wind. On the other side of the water the few willow trees left us by the Thames Conservancy looked doubtfully alive against the bleak sky and the row of wretched-looking blue-slated houses, although, by the way, the latter were the backs of a sort of street of "villas" and not a slum; the road in front of the house was sooty and muddy at once, and in the air was that sense of dirty discomfort which one is never quit of in London. The morning was harsh, too, and though the wind was from the southwest it was as cold as a north wind; and yet amidst it all, I thought of the corner of the next bight of the river which I could not quite see from where I was, but over which one can see clear of houses and into Richmond Park, looking like the open country; and dirty as the river was, and harsh as was the January wind, they seemed to woo me toward the countryside, where away from the miseries of the "Great Wen" I might of my own will carry on a daydream of the friends I had made in the dream of the night and against my will.

But as I turned away shivering and downhearted, on a sudden came the frightful noise of the "hooters," one after the other, that call the workmen to the factories, this one the after-breakfast one, more by token. So I grinned surlily, and dressed and got ready for my day's "work" as I call it, but which many a man besides John Ruskin (though not many in his position) would call "play."

Chapter XIII

A KING'S LESSON

*I*t is told of Matthias Corvinus, king of Hungary — the Alfred the Great of his time and people — that he once heard (once *only?*) that some (only *some,* my lad?) of his peasants were overworked and under-fed. So he sent for his Council, and bade come thereto also some of the mayors of the good towns, and some of the lords of land and their bailiffs, and asked them of the truth thereof; and in diverse ways they all told one and the same tale, how the peasant carles were stout and well able to work and had enough and to spare of meat and drink, seeing that they were but churls; and how if they worked not at the least as hard as they did, it would be ill for them and ill for their lords; for that the more the churl hath the more he asketh; and that when he knoweth wealth, he knoweth the lack of it also, as it fared with our first parents in the Garden of God. The King sat and said but little while they spake, but he misdoubted them that they were liars. So the Council brake up with nothing done; but the King took the matter to heart, being, as kings go, a just man, besides being more valiant than they mostly were, even in the old feudal time. So within two or three days, says the tale, he called together such lords and councilors as he deemed fittest, and bade busk them for a ride; and when they were ready he and they set out, over rough and smooth, decked out in all the glory of attire which was the wont of those days. Thus they rode till they came to some village or thorpe of the peasant folk, and through it to the vineyards where men were working on the sunny southern slopes that went up from the river: my tale does not say whether that were Theiss, or Donau, or what river. Well, I judge it was late spring or early summer, and the vines but just beginning to show their grapes; for the vintage is late in those lands, and some of the grapes are not gathered till the first frosts have touched them, whereby the wine made from them is the stronger and sweeter. Anyhow there were the peasants, men and women, boys and young maidens, toiling and swinking; some hoeing between the vine-rows, some bearing baskets of dung up the steep slopes, some in one way, some in another, laboring for the fruit they should never eat, and the wine they should never drink. Thereto turned the King and got off his horse and began to climb up the stony ridges of the vineyard, and his lords in like manner followed him, wondering in their hearts what was toward; but to the one who was following next after him he turned about and said with a smile, "Yea, lords, this is a new game we are playing today, and a new knowledge will come from it." And the lord smiled, but somewhat sourly.

As for the peasants, great was their fear of those gay and golden lords. I judge that they did not know the King, since it was little likely that any one of them had seen his face; and they knew of him but as the Great

Father, the mighty warrior who kept the Turk from harrying their thorpe. Though, forsooth, little matter was it to any man there whether Turk or Magyar was their overlord, since to one master or another they had to pay the due tale of laboring days in the year, and hard was the livelihood that they earned for themselves on the days when they worked for themselves and their wives and children.

Well, belike they knew not the King; but amidst those rich lords they saw and knew their own lord, and of him they were sore afraid. But naught it availed them to flee away from those strong men and strong horses — they who had been toiling from before the rising of the sun, and now it wanted little more than an hour of noon: besides, with the King and lords was a guard of crossbowmen, who were left the other side of the vineyard wall, — keen-eyed Italians of the mountains, straight shooters of the bolt. So the poor folk fled not; nay they made as if all this were none of their business, and went on with their work. For indeed each man said to himself, "If I be the one that is not slain, tomorrow I shall lack bread if I do not work my hardest today; and maybe I shall be headman if some of these be slain and I live."

Now comes the King amongst them and says: "Good fellows, which of you is the headman?"

Spake a man, sturdy and sunburned, well on in years and grizzled: "I am the headman, lord."

"Give me thy hoe, then," says the King; "for now shall I order this matter myself, since these lords desire a new game, and are fain to work under me at vine-dressing. But do thou stand by me and set me right if I order them wrong: but the rest of you go play!"

The carle knew not what to think, and let the King stand with his hand stretched out, while he looked askance at his own lord and baron, who wagged his head at him grimly as one who says, "Do it, dog!"

Then the carle lets the hoe come into the King's hand; and the King falls to, and orders his lords for vine-dressing, to each his due share of the work: and whiles the carle said yea and whiles nay to his ordering. And then ye should have seen velvet cloaks cast off, and mantles of fine Flemish scarlet go to the dusty earth; as the lords and knights busked them to the work.

So they buckled to; and to most of them it seemed good game to play at vine-dressing. But one there was who, when his scarlet cloak was off, stood up in a doublet of glorious Persian web of gold and silk, such as men make not now, worth a hundred florins the Bremen ell. Unto him the King with no smile on his face gave the job of toing and froing up and down the hill with the biggest and the frailest dung-basket that there was; and thereat the silken lord screwed up a grin, that was sport to see, and all the lords laughed; and as he turned away he said, yet so that none heard him, "Do I serve this son's son of a whore that he should bid me carry dung?" For you must know that the King's father, John Hunyad, one of the great warriors of the world, the Hammer of the Turks, was not gotten in wedlock, though he were a king's son.

Well, they sped the work bravely for a while, and loud was the laughter as the hoes smote the earth and the flint stones tinkled and the cloud of dust rose up; the brocaded dung-bearer went up and down, cursing and swearing by the White God and the Black; and one would say to another, "See ye how gentle blood outgoes churls' blood, even when the gentle does the churl's work: these lazy loons smote but one stroke to our three." But the King, who worked no worse than any, laughed not at all; and meanwhile the poor folk stood by, not daring to speak a word one to the other; for they were still sore afraid, not now of being slain on the spot, but this rather was in their hearts: "These great and strong lords and knights have come to see what work a man may do without dying: if we are to have yet more days added to our year's tale of lords' labor, then are we lost without remedy." And their hearts sank within them.

So sped the work; and the sun rose yet higher in the heavens, and it was noon and more. And now there was no more laughter among those toiling lords, and the strokes of the hoe and mattock came far slower, while the dung-bearer sat down at the bottom of the hill and looked out on the river; but the King yet worked on doggedly, so for shame the other lords yet kept at it. Till at last the next man to the King let his hoe drop with a clatter, and swore a great oath. Now he was a strong black-bearded man in the prime of life, a valiant captain of that famous Black Band that had so often rent the Turkish array; and the King loved him for his sturdy valor; so he says to him, "Is aught wrong, Captain?"

"Nay, lord," says he, "ask the headman carle yonder what ails us."

"Headman," says the King, "what ails these strong knights? Have I ordered them wrongly?"

"Nay, but shirking ails them, lord," says he, "for they are weary; and no wonder, for they have been playing hard, and are of gentle blood."

"Is that so, lord," says the King, "that ye are weary already?"

Then the rest hung their heads and said naught, all save that captain of war; and he said, being a bold man and no liar: "King, I see what thou wouldst be at; thou hast brought us here to preach us a sermon from that Plato of thine; and to say sooth, so that I may swink no more, and go eat my dinner, now preach thy worst!

Nay, if thou wilt be priest I will be thy deacon. Wilt thou that I ask this laboring carle a thing or two?"

"Yea," said the King. And there came, as it were, a cloud of thought over his face.

Then the captain straddled his legs and looked big, and said to the carle: "Good fellow, how long have we been working here?"

"Two hours or thereabout, judging by the sun above us," says he.

"And how much of thy work have we done in that while?" says the captain, and winks his eye at him withal.

"Lord," says the carle, grinning a little despite himself, "be not wroth with my word. In the first half-hour ye did five-and-forty minutes' work of ours, and in the next half-hour scant a thirty minutes' work, and the third half-hour a fifteen minutes' work, and in the fourth half-hour two minutes' work." The grin now had faded from his face, but a gleam came into his eyes as he said: "And now, as I suppose, your day's work is done, and ye will go to your dinner, and eat the sweet and drink the strong; and we shall eat a little rye-bread, and then be working here till after the sun has set and the moon has begun to cast shadows. Now for you, I wot not how ye shall sleep nor where, nor what white body ye shall hold in your arms while the night flits and the stars shine; but for us, while the stars yet shine, shall we be at it again, and bethink ye for what! I know not what game and play ye shall be devising for tomorrow as ye ride back home; but for us when we come back here tomorrow, it shall be as if there had been no yesterday and nothing done therein, and that work of that today shall be naught to us also, for we shall win no respite from our toil thereby, and the morrow of tomorrow will all be to begin again once more, and so on and on till no tomorrow abideth us. Therefore, if ye are thinking to lay some new tax or tale upon us, think twice of it, for we may not bear it. And all this I say with the less fear, because I perceive this man here beside me, in the black velvet jerkin and the gold chain on his neck, is the King; nor do I think he will slay me for my word since he hath so many a Turk before him and his mighty sword!"

Then said the captain: "Shall I smite the man, O King? or hath he preached thy sermon for thee?"

"Smite not, for he hath preached it," said the King. "Hearken to the carle's sermon, lords and councilors of mine! Yet when another hath spoken our thought, other thoughts are born therefrom, and now have I another sermon to preach; but I will refrain me as now. Let us down and to our dinner."

So they went, the King and his gentles, and sat down by the river under the rustle of the poplars, and they ate and drank and were merry. And the King bade bear up the broken meats to the vine-dressers, and a good draft of the archer's wine, and to the headman he gave a broad gold piece, and to each man three silver pennies. But when the poor folk had all that under their hands, it was to them as though the kingdom of heaven had come down to earth.

In the cool of the evening home rode the King and his lords. The King was distraught and silent; but at last the captain, who rode beside him, said to him: "Preach me now thine after-sermon, O King!"

"I think thou knowest it already," said the King, "else hadst thou not spoken in such wise to the carle; but tell me what is thy craft and the craft of all these, whereby ye live, as the potter by making pots, and so forth?"

Said the captain: "As the potter lives by making pots, so we live by robbing the poor."

Again said the King: "And my trade?"

Said he, "Thy trade is to be a king of such thieves, yet no worser than the rest."

The King laughed.

"Bear that in mind," said he, "and then shall I tell thee my thought while yonder carle spake. 'Carle,' I thought, 'were I thou or such as thou, then would I take in my hand a sword or a spear, or were it only a hedge-stake, and bid others do the like, and forth would we go; and since we would be so many, and with naught to lose save a miserable life, we would do battle and pre vail, and make an end of the craft of kings and of lords and of usurers, and there should be but one craft in the world, to wit, to work merrily for ourselves and to live merrily thereby.'"

Said the captain: "This then is thy sermon. Who will heed it if thou preach it?"

Said the King: "They who will take the mad king and put him in a king's madhouse, therefore do I forbear to preach it. Yet it *shall* be preached."

"And not heeded," said the captain, "save by those who head and hang the setters forth of new things that are good for the world. Our trade is safe for many an many a generation."

And therewith they came to the King's palace, and they ate and drank and slept and the world went on its ways.